ROXANNE PULITZER

SIMON & SCHUSTER

Facade

A Novel

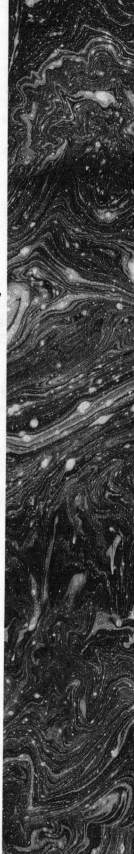

New York   London   Toronto   Sydney   Tokyo   Singapore

SIMON & SCHUSTER
Simon & Schuster Building
Rockefeller Center
1230 Avenue of the Americas
New York, New York 10020

Designed by Caroline Cunningham

Manufactured in the United States of America

1   3   5   7   9   10   8   6   4   2

Library of Congress Cataloging-in-Publication Data
Pulitzer, Roxanne.
Facade/Roxanne Pulitzer.
p.   cm.
I. Title.
PS3566.U38F3   1992
813'.54—dc20   92–11932
CIP
ISBN 0-671-74332-5

To Mac and Zac.
You two are always my inspiration.

$\mathcal{P}$ROLOGUE

Summer 1990

$\mathcal{M}$aria could not distinguish his face, yet she knew he was the King of Spades. Her feeling was of water and darkness, and that she was so heavy she couldn't move. She looked down over his lifeless body in the Intensive Care Unit and wondered whether this man would be saved. An emergency CAT scan showed massive swelling of the brain. An artificial lung machine was breathing for him.

Maria felt the first flicker of pain course through her body.

He lay flat and motionless, as monitors beeped and buzzed. Several IV tubes gave him fluids and medication.

Something swept through her, hot as lightning.

A doctor was trying to thread a small catheter into an artery so he could get an exact reading of the oxygen in his blood.

Suddenly, Maria was moving very fast even though there was no wind blowing on her face. . . . She was back in her body. . . . The police folder she had been holding was back on the desk and her hands were clasped on top of it as if she could hold the folder's secrets in place. Her eyes were brimming with concern.

She had just finished reading the cards for Kate, Sarah, Jessie, and Christine. She removed her glasses and gulped in the scent of the rosewater lotion she had soaked herself in earlier that day. The aromatic oil energized her. She must get back to work.

Maria was sitting at the mahogany desk in her living room. The small room was furnished with a luxurious disorder peculiar to the psychic. There were books piled everywhere, and the fragrance of flowers from the garden filled the air. The late afternoon was humid, as only West Palm Beach afternoons can be.

She had been busily writing notes to herself, sorting detective reports of missing children into neat stacks, solved and unsolved, bundling them together with rubber bands. Tomorrow she was to be honored for twenty-five years of service to the Police Department. Just last week she had located a five-year-old boy who had been kidnapped. The best part of Maria, the jewel stuck deep inside her core, was determination to help people.

She sighed and began rubbing at her temples, where her hair was mostly gray. She was tall, thin, and refined. Her eyes were bright and startlingly clear. Thin lines crisscrossed her high cheekbones and her forehead, reflecting her almost seventy years.

The police work kept her so busy she didn't read the cards as much anymore on an individual basis as she once had. But today, she couldn't keep her mind off the four women and the King of Spades. Who was he? She had known the girls for over ten years now. They belonged to the selective group of clients she still read for regularly. The four of them were wedded by brilliance, talent, and secrets—but what made them close friends was that they were father's girls without fathers. The silent pain of that was their greatest bond.

Usually, they came separately; however, once a year they would all show up together. Today, they had been consumed by a terrible fear of danger in each of their readings from the same man. He was represented by the King of Spades.

A dull throbbing weight of pain encircled her head like a crown of thorns. Hatred; a nervous terror shook her from head to toe. The knots of lies and deception the girls had perpetrated over the years were getting tangled tighter and tighter, threatening to strangle them all.

Maria was aware, only too well, of human weakness and failings—and the limitations imposed by the physical bodies in which we dwell. She did not want to be regarded as an authority, and had never wanted to become a crutch for anyone to lean on. Her earnest desire and purpose was that she could act as the spark that would ignite the flames of one's own intuition, so one could answer one's own questions.

Under her desk, she crossed her long thin legs and tapped one foot. The faint smell of jasmine wafted in on a thin damp breeze, reminding her of her childhood in Hungary, her daily walks with her governess, into the wooded area behind the family chateau. There was a band of gypsies who had lived along the river for years, but to her dismay, she had never been allowed to play with them. That was strictly forbidden.

"Give me salt ... give me salt," the children always begged whenever they passed by.

Maria's heart had fluttered that particular day, because she had secretly gathered salt from the kitchen for weeks. She rarely broke the rules, but this was very important to her. In her jacket pocket was a damask napkin filled with her efforts. She peeked cautiously to either side of her, then quickly pushed a tightly folded piece of linen into the hands of a little girl, as her nanny strolled on ahead. Suddenly, all of the children's eyes squinched up in laughter, grins spreading across their faces.

"It's salt, Mama," they squealed. "Look, look. It's salt."

Maria felt her shoulder blades draw tightly together and the weight of blood in her hands, as tears fell down her cheeks. How could she have known that the gypsy children were asking for money in their traditional way.

Their laughter seemed to go on forever. Heat pulsed through her body and pulled at her stomach like needles. In her heart a dam broke.

"Come to me, little one," said a plump woman with lines like railroad tracks on her skin, the color of a paper bag. "For your generosity, I give you my only treasure."

The woman moved in closer, wrapping Maria in soft words, soft hands. Her eyes stared straight into Maria's, as she grabbed her shoulders, squeezing them tightly with her thick fingers.

Maria could feel her dress sticking to her body.

"You will see the future," she whispered. Her words fell like soft pieces of flower petals. Maria simply nodded. She chose not to say anything, because deep inside she knew.

Maria gasped for air now—she was drowning in a sea of knowing. That had been the summer of her ninth year.

Johann Strauss was playing in the background, yet Maria wasn't enjoying his music as much as usual. She couldn't free her mind of the four women. There were ominous crossings of fate with all of them, and the King of Spades. She turned from the window and looked into the mirror as she untied her French twist. Maria did not see herself. She did not hear the music. She felt the pressure of dead stillness against her eardrums. She saw the silhouette of a woman standing over the King of Spades in the hospital. The woman was faceless.

Maria pressed her forehead to the glass and tried not to think. She concentrated on the relief of the mirror's cooling touch, forcing her mind into blankness.

"It is finally over," said a voice as cold as a skeleton, naked of emotion.

Maria shook her head violently, opening her eyes. She stepped back from the mirror, away from the hatred. It frightened her. She knew the woman.

The King of Spades was floating face down in the swimming pool.

"Oh my God . . . Murder."

Part One

1980s

CHAPTER 1

QUEEN OF CLUBS:
Ruled by her mind

*C*hristine Wells maneuvered her Audi through the London streets that were swarming with taxis and double-decker buses. It was a typical London afternoon, the air soft, gray, and wet. She was on her way to see Mark Althorp, who was 70 miles northwest of London in the heart of Northamptonshire. He was a man of habit and she knew tea would be served promptly at five o'clock on a beautiful sterling silver tea service, with delicious cakes, tinned biscuits from Fortnum and Mason's, and a slightly tart orange marmalade. She stepped on the gas pedal. She was starving.

Christine was a tall, slender, wispy creature, in her mid-twenties, pale-skinned with enormous light green eyes, which could look alternatively grave and preoccupied, or merry. She was a contradictory character, her physical frailty belying an abundance of nervous energy. Today her eyes were subtly lined with warm grays, and her mane of honey blonde curls tumbled and tangled around her beautiful face. She had high cheekbones, and her full lips were tinted with the most sensuous shade of deep pink, shiny and glossed.

She checked her classically chiseled features in the rear-view mirror. Christine had an unforgettable smile, which she knew. Her teeth were so white, so perfectly straight, they were startling. There was a mole above the right side of her lip that was perfectly round as if the work of an eyebrow pencil. She was exceptionally good-looking. In her line of work, she needed to be.

Christine had run away from home in Australia at age eighteen with a girlfriend, one of thousands of young Australians who poured into the Earl's Court district of London in the late sixties. She knew deep down inside her that she wanted more than what her working-class family had planned for her future. She had always pictured herself married to one of the grand old doges from Venice's heyday, lolling around in a sumptuous palazzo, attired in reams of finery. There was no way she could get there from small-town Australia.

Her schooling was sketchy, consisting of correspondence courses and lessons on the radio in Sydney, and a few years at a public school. She had arrived in England with only her face as her fortune, and like a small cyclone, had pounded the pavement trying to find work as an actress. But the competition was tremendous. Instead, without meaning to be flighty, she worked her way through many short-lived careers—modeling for underwear and toothpaste ads, becoming a one-time seller of silver antiques on London's Portobello Road, dressing mannequins. She made money easily, but never felt she had enough. She had not been in London long when one afternoon, while trying to hail a taxi in the rain, she was picked up in Belgravia Square by a man who hooted at her from his car, and introduced her to Simone. Simone changed her life. Simone owned and ran a small, very exclusive "hotel."

Christine did not enjoy the sex—it was strictly work to her. In the beginning, she had had a few dreadful, painful, and humiliating experiences, but not many. Primarily, throughout the first year, she worked together with her Australian girlfriend.

They knew each other's bodies as intimately as they knew their own, but loved each other simply as sisters. However, one night a man handled them both roughly, and her friend returned to Australia. Christine turned to Simone until she could save enough to strike out alone.

Christine knew she had to elevate herself to a higher clientele to survive on her own, so she spent her hard-earned money on first-class train seats to Paris because she knew she wouldn't meet anybody in second-class, and her gambles began to pay off. Yet, she knew she needed to do something more. She wanted houses, fabulous jewels, couture clothes; wanted to travel on private planes and yachts, like she read about, so she enlisted Simone's help.

Simone found her a diction teacher to rid her of her provincial accent and any harsh tones, until she spoke softly and mellifluously. She hired tutors to teach her about the arts and sent her to all the latest plays. She plied her with the latest biographies and books on philosophy. She paid for lessons in manners, etiquette, wine, and foods. Christine was quick to learn, and at the end of a six-month course, she had covered almost everything. She invented a new background for herself without the poverty, and didn't bother to stay in touch with her real family. They had never been close so this was no real sacrifice. She went to all the right parties, and was busy from dusk till dawn. She was dazzling, and strangely classless, fitting in anywhere.

Christine had learned how to use her assets to the utmost until she became the one in control. Now, she was only available for special clients: rich ones.

There was the Englishman who liked her to spank him because of the way he had been brought up, with a sadistic nanny who always paddled him, and the boarding school where he had been caned for the master's pleasure. Now he couldn't live without the pain.

There was the older American who loved her youth and made her dress up in a prep school outfit—a white skirt, blue blazer, long white socks, and black flat shoes; the Frenchman who liked to watch her with another man. They all kept her in a lifestyle about which she had dreamed and now had become accustomed to.

Then there was Mark. . . .

The rain had turned to a fine mist again as Christine headed up the oak-lined driveway. Long grasses were cut with narrow mown paths that led to walled gardens surrounding the house. She stepped out of the car with graceful certainty and headed up the side entrance where there were wooden garden seats bleached to ashy gray from being left out through many English winters. To one side, an ancient wooden pergola supported a tangled mass of pink roses. A butler, tall and discreet in black tails and striped gray trousers, opened the door. He was a dignified, white-haired man whose noncommittal expression never changed. As he showed her in, she gazed around a moment, awed as always by the massive red-brick building that once had had a moat around it and dated from the 1400s. Inside, she knew, it was beautifully furnished with French antiques and brocade curtains. There were sweeping stairs, paneled halls, gleaming parquet floors, and priceless Oriental rugs. A 110-square foot gallery upstairs held a treasury of museum-quality Impressionist art.

She sighed. It was so perfect.

When she was growing up, red bricks of her street melted into uniformity of look-alike doors and brownstone steps. The similarity had been unsettling. She remembered coming home one day, panic rumbling through her.

"Which one is our house, Grandma? Which one?"

"One-five-five," she had said, pointing to the chipped number painted next to the door.

"They are all alike," cried Christine. "The same brick, the same backyard, the same color."

"The real difference is inside," her grandmother had replied.

She hadn't known whether or not to believe that. She wanted one with a white picket fence and flowers . . . where a happy family lived.

That afternoon, she crossed six blocks, leaving behind bricks and litter-filled streets, emerging at a street where there were brilliant flowers, clean walkways, and robins flying overhead. The only birds in her neighborhood were pigeons. There had been a faint twinge of sadness within her, a drop of pain moving briefly and vanishing like raindrops on windows.

The butler discreetly showed Christine into the master bedroom and left her there, alone, to wait. She was dressed demurely in a short black silk dress with spiky black high heels that showed off her superb legs. Ever since she had first started to buy her own clothes as a teenager, she had liked black for the drama it created. The skin on her face and arms was like porcelain. Her waist was tiny, her hips gloriously curved. The sheerness of the dress outlined the roundness of her full breasts, making it breathtakingly obvious she wore no bra. But it was not only these attributes that made her sexy: She exuded a sensuousness as strong as a cloud of perfume.

Slowly pacing the plush white carpet, she lighted a cigarette that she took out of a silver Cartier case—a gift from a pleased client. The soft lights of the chandelier cast a dreamy incandescence over the objects in the room, and Christine felt herself becoming engulfed by the romantic ambience. She thought of Mark and the hours ahead with him.

She had been "introduced" to the American at a party in an elegant apartment in Kensington. Their second meeting was in a suite at Blake's. After that, they met at the house.

He was in his mid-thirties, and strikingly handsome with very dark hair and eyes. He had made a fortune in something or other, and came into London at least once a month on business. The staff kept the house running like a precision machine even in his absence. He was well over six feet, broad-shouldered yet slender, and always very well dressed. What was his wife like? Where was she?

Would any of them ever leave their wives?

How nice it would be, she thought wistfully, to have a

real relationship, to have children with someone, grow old with someone. She tried to stop such thoughts. They served no useful purpose. She wasn't allowed to wonder or ask. She simply had to do what she was paid to do. Simone's words rang in her ears.

"Many men are starved for love and affection—and while they can't expect to buy love, we can certainly offer the affection." Christine didn't believe in love anyway. To her, it was merely infatuation—it never lasted, and certainly had nothing to do with marriage.

Mark entered the bedroom soundlessly. He was in gray flannel trousers, a blue shirt, and a gold-buttoned navy blazer. He strode over to the liquor cart and lifted a decanter filled with amber liquid.

No matter what the circumstances, he insisted that she be masked. The mask was in place now. She regarded him through the eye holes. Black eyes surrounded by black lace in a black mask.

The light from candles next to the bed seemed to undulate and shift. He walked toward her, crystal glasses in his hands. His fingers were long and strong. Lover's fingers, she thought. He wore a gold nugget ring carved with a family crest on his right hand.

They stood for a long moment in silence, looking at each other.

"You're beautiful today," he said.

Her smile lifted her mask slightly.

He stood close to her, putting down the drinks. She was struck by his familiar scent. He had worn it previous times. He always insisted she never mute her natural woman scent with perfume. "A woman's scent is like her fingerprints, hers alone," he had explained.

"Tell me what you want," she whispered.

"I want you to do anything—and everything. . . ." he replied.

She put her arms gently around his waist, while one thigh slipped between his legs and moved ever so slowly forward and backward. She pressed against him with a passion he paid for, although with him she felt . . . something.

His hand came to her cheek, then traced the edge of her mask. There was nothing hurried in him. He bent his head and touched his lips lightly to her ear.

He began to work the zipper at the back of her dress, kissing her neck all the while and holding her against him. The top half of her dress came down. She knew it was the contrast he liked, the severity of the black, and the half-naked body.

She raised his face and flicked her tongue along his neck and in his ear while he stood there. She lowered her dress to the floor, tantalizing in black satin and lace, and silk stockings, then undid his belt and removed his trousers. With skillful hands, she drew him out, stroking him.

Placing his hands on her shoulders, he pressed her down until she was kneeling. He watched her take him into her mouth. Her tongue circled him, teasing him.

Lifting her suddenly, he carried her to the bed and sat her down, facing him. Her hands, warm and tentative, fluttered over his skin like butterflies, while she kissed his stomach and chest. When he groaned, she lingered there on his nipples.

She pulled him down to the bed, kissing, stroking, and then she lay on top of him. When his hand slid down between her legs, she brought it back up wordlessly.

She got up on her elbows, straddling him, her long hair

teasing him with its softness on his chest. She looked down at him through the black mask. He was caught in those intense eyes. She then gently raked her long fingernails down his chest, up the inside of his thighs, until he quivered with desire.

Christine loved this precise moment when she was filled with power, *her* own power.

She took his erection in her hand and moved gently now, inserting him slowly, so as not to bring him to completion too soon.

She bent forward and pressed her mouth to his, something she had never done before. She never kissed.

As she raised up on her hands, he was held by her gaze. She slowly rode up and down, squeezing him, then retracting with her muscles until he was bursting with desire.

"Come," she urged. "Fill me."

He moved rapidly now, his strong hands holding her tightly to his hardness. He closed his eyes. Finally, he shuddered, groaned, pulling her down so hard that she felt the sharpness of both pleasure and pain. It took her breath away.

Mark watched Christine stride naked to the window. She drew back the dark blue velvet curtains for a peek outside, then closed them again. Standing framed against the drapes, her blonde beauty took on an unearthly quality. She was a living, breathing invitation to debauchery, he thought; to adventure and sophisticated revelry.

A cigarette hung limply in his hand. He didn't notice it. His thoughts went to his wife. She came from an old family that had both money and position, but the marriage was of convenience only.

He crossed the room, his eyes on Christine. There were always women available to slake his needs, but Christine was different. She ignited him. She intrigued him. No matter that she was paid well to make him feel good, he desired her as he never had any other woman.

He kissed her violently.

"I'm taking you back to Palm Beach with me."

"What about your wife?"

"My wife is very busy with her circle of friends. I've given her none of my time for months."

Christine's huge eyes flamed with excitement, and her porcelain cheeks flushed pink. She hugged him hard.

"It will be wonderful, Mark. I'll make you very happy."

"That's the whole point of paying you, Christine. To guarantee you make me happy," he said with unnecessary cruelty.

But Christine said nothing, and they both knew that while Mark might foot the bills, it was Christine's sexual power that was in control.

There were occasions these days when Simone couldn't stand the company of fashionable London. She had been a part of it for twenty years and she told herself she was getting too rich, too comfortable, and too old to be bothered to make the effort to be charming all the time. So now more and more often she would banish the gentlemen who still sought her company, have her chef cook a lavish dinner, and invite Christine. As was their habit, they would share a bottle of champagne, and talk over the happenings of recent nights.

Simone was drinking her fourth glass of Dom Pérignon, and listening to Christine repeat how wonderful Mark was to take her with him to America.

Simone snuggled back against the pale blue damask of her chair, one arm resting on the gilt frame above her head. She knew it was a striking pose that Christine would appreciate, then emulate. When the two had first met, Simone had been flattered by Christine's adoration, and she loved Christine, but tonight she was fast running out of patience.

"There's nothing new you can tell me about what happens between the sheets, Christine," she began. "You had better put all that romantic nonsense behind you, and settle for a comfortable relationship, where *you* have the upper hand."

"This is going to be different," exclaimed Christine, her beautiful face shining with vitality. "It's a new beginning, Simone. There will be no other men for me, only Mark. He isn't happy with his wife. Maybe he'll leave her."

Simone glanced at her shrewdly. "Isn't it rather odd he didn't leave you a phone number where you could reach him?"

"He sent me a plane ticket, and promised he'd pick me up at the airport," Christine told her. "Besides, he has sole responsibility for an enormous business; he's probably traveling," she added defensively.

"For all your sophisticated appearance and experience, my dear, you are still naive and unworldly."

"So you think I shouldn't leave?"

"I didn't say that," Simone said. She got up and went over to where Christine was standing by the French doors that led to a little courtyard. "You don't need me anymore, Christine, no matter what happens."

Simone reflected back to one of their first intimate talks. She had questioned Christine about her background. When her father's name had come up, it caused a violent reaction.

"I'm scared of him. I was always scared of him. He used to beat me up. He knocked out my front tooth. He broke my nose. I was in the hospital for ten days thanks to him." She had struggled not to cry. "My mother came to visit me in the hospital. She told me if I told anyone, Daddy would beat her up."

Simone had had to reassure her that violence was not permitted in her hotel. It had taken her two years to convince Christine that spanking was exciting to customers and not considered violent. She had prepared her well for life as a pleasure-giving, sensitive, understanding courtesan. She hoped that life would treat her well, but this trip with Mark did not feel right to Simone. Still, there was nothing left to teach, nothing left to advise. Sooner or later Christine had to go off on her own. And that time was now.

Christine's things were packed and she was ready to leave. She stared soberly around the apartment that had been like a home to her for over five years.

"Good luck, my friend," Simone said now. "And good-bye."

CHAPTER 2

QUEEN OF HEARTS:
Ruled by emotions

*I*t was Monday morning and Kate Robinson was sitting on the edge of the bathtub waiting for Lisa Greene, her roommate, to finish brushing her teeth. She felt the cold porcelain through her nightshirt. Lisa stared at her smile in the medicine cabinet mirror, then rinsed her mouth three times with the strong red mouthwash, making the whole bathroom smell like a dentist's office. Lisa kept smiling and examining herself in the mirror.

"Hurry up," said Kate, exasperated. "You're going to make me late for work."

Kate hated roommates. She hated winters. Would her boss

ROXANNE PULITZER

give her the assignment in Palm Beach? It would mean staying in Florida for three whole months writing about vacationing celebrities. She thought of the warmth, and the privacy.

Once a year, when Kate was growing up, she and her parents used to drive out in the summer to Atlantic City from their cramped Bronx apartment. They would go to the beach, get out their thermoses and their sandwiches, and Kate would always say, "Oh, I want a house overlooking the ocean—I'm going to buy myself one."

"I want, I want," her father would chide, "that's all you ever say. You're too selfish, Kate."

New York had always seemed cold and bleak to her. She didn't have good memories of her childhood. Everyone had always been very busy getting on with surviving; there had been no time for luxuries like warmth. She had left home at sixteen and still had nightmares about going back to the Bronx.

"Your father called yesterday," Lisa said, putting on bright pink lipstick.

"Oh yeah?" Kate responded, as if it were no big deal, as if it happened every week, instead of once in a blue moon.

Kate never talked about her father. She was good at pretending not to care. Real good. She never said she missed her father or wanted to see him.

"No message. Said he'd call again," Lisa told her. Then: "Your turn," and she left the bathroom to Kate.

One glance in the mirror and Kate saw the hungry look in her eyes for her father. Her father was a forklift driver with a barrel-like body, iron-gray hair. Her mother had been seriously injured in an automobile accident when Kate was a toddler. Kate had never known her, except as a 90-pound paraplegic.

30

Kate remembered one afternoon when she had gone shopping with her mother. She liked shopping; liked standing in front of a mirror, feeling a new dress against her skin, and dreaming of where she could wear her beautiful new outfit. Her father was sitting in the living room when they returned, and Kate sashayed past him, twirling and whirling around after she changed into her new clothes. Her father stared, then squinted at her in such a way that Kate's hands went immediately to her head, as if her hair was mussed up. He said nothing, so Kate continued to model her dress. She loved her father desperately. He was one of those very masculine men who loomed large. If he said something wasn't correct, then her whole world came tumbling down around her. He wasn't nice, he wasn't kind, but he was strong and forceful and *big.*

"You like that outfit?" her father asked in such a way it was clear he didn't. "You look fat in it. You have no class at all," he went on, shaking his head in disapproval. "You'll never amount to anything."

Something pinched inside her chest when she heard those words.

"I can be good at whatever I want," she retorted, sticking her chin out a little. "I'll show you, I'm going to be a famous writer," she added quickly.

Kate looked at him, as if searching for something. Please, please, please believe in me. Please, please, please love me.

"You can't write . . . you couldn't spell your way out of a paper bag!"

Each word her father uttered stood at attention as if doing battle in a war to be heard.

"I'll show you," she said with a sudden, almost proud ferocity.

"Humph," was his only reply, his expansive belly heaving

threateningly against the dangerously thin belt around his waist.

"Don't mind him, he doesn't mean it, Katie," said her mother. She clutched her leg, which had started twitching with an involuntary muscle spasm. "He's had too much to drink. His words are *never* to be taken seriously when he drinks."

Kate stood on the bracers on the back of the wheelchair, and placed her arms around her mother's neck.

"I am always going to take care of you," Kate whispered.

"I am not *your* responsibility, darling," her mother said in a loving tone, as smooth as cherry cough syrup. "I want you to look after yourself. Please don't worry about me, I'll go right on, the same as I always have."

Nothing could put a dent in her mother's dignity. She was a woman who took her Catholic duty very seriously. She did volunteer work with the senior citizens' group at the church, playing canasta and pinochle with them by the hour. She was also on the school board and the prison board, all dignified pursuits, all remarkable achievements for a crippled woman.

"Please help me to my bath, Katie."

Mrs. Robinson was so tiny, Kate didn't have much trouble. She hoisted her from her wheelchair into the warm water. She smiled serenely at Kate for a brief moment, her face full of sunshine.

———

"Coffee is ready," Lisa shouted.

Kate dropped her Maybelline mascara in the sink. "Damn."

Kate had a pale cream complexion and shoulder-length

bleached-blonde hair that was straight and lustrous. Her nose was tiny and pug, and she had a character line that ran straight across her high forehead. She was five-seven, with a voluptuous body. In her mind, she was too voluptuous, and always five pounds overweight. However, when she had to, she knew the clothes to accentuate her figure and would make it a practice to wear them, although she preferred to wear loose pants and big jackets.

Kate could make herself up to be stunning and was generally regarded as a beautiful woman by most everyone. Only her eyes were not pretty. They were too far apart, neither quite blue nor green, and empty of warmth.

All her life, Kate had been self-sufficient. She was never liked at school. She never had a best friend. Kate's trouble was her independent nature. She was too forthright in her opinions, abrasively streetwise, and too stubbornly resistant to any kind of rules. She knew she had no time to think *what if*. . . . You just got on with it. Whatever she did, she just wanted to be number one.

Kate had dropped out of City College during her sophomore year, devastated by the death of her mother. Her memories of her were vivid. Never once had she witnessed her mother mourn the life she had. Her mother had been the one who held the family together. Since her death, five years ago, Kate heard very little from her father, unless *she* went to see him, and that she did only once a year, on the anniversary of her mother's death. Her father was too negative, too destructive, and though she knew better, his criticism could still pain her. The only way to move ahead with her life was to avoid him.

She would survive it. She was able to survive it because she did not believe in suffering. She refused to let it matter.

Suffering was senseless. It was not to be part of her life, as she saw it. She would not allow the pain to become important. She sent him a monthly check, as she always had ever since she moved out. "He doesn't matter." The words ran through her mind. An immovable certainty within kept repeating, "I am somebody. . . . I am somebody."

"Thanks for the note under my door last night abandoning me to my room," Lisa said as she gave Kate a cup of black coffee. Kate always left a note taped to the bathroom mirror when one of her dates was going to last all night.

"Sorry," Kate responded, trying to put her mouth into a proper expression of regret; she succeeded only in betraying that the process was an effort. Lisa had no boyfriends of her own, and Kate thought often that was why Lisa was such a good writer. Her life was lived vicariously and Kate always had the feeling her roommate was watching her as if from a distance, gathering details. It made Kate feel uncomfortable and jealous at the same time.

Kate was forever getting rid of Lisa whenever one of her boyfriends was around. She was twenty-three years old, and dating a variety of men, and none of them knew about each other: a singer, a photographer, the manager of a rock group.

Kate smiled to herself. With the photographer, it was over each time almost before it started. With the singer, it was romantic, but unsatisfying. With the manager of the rock group, it was passion and carnality.

Kate liked sex. She just did not want any involvement that would complicate her life and deflect her from what she was going to do. She played the game for connections, not love. Her ambition was to be independent and successful. Anything or anybody who helped her achieve those goals— great. What impeded her would be eliminated.

"So who was it last night?"

"Mike Slatkin."

"The newscaster? You went to bed with him?" Lisa asked, her cheeks turning pink with embarrassment.

"Why, what's wrong?"

"Oh, nothing."

"Don't give me 'oh nothing,' " Kate persisted.

"I heard he has a huge you-know-what."

"You heard right. By the way, you-know-whats are called penises!" Kate said, roaring with laughter.

Lisa was an unattractive girl with fair skin and light brown hair that she wore too short. She stood barely five feet tall, with a prominent nose and dark circles under her eyes. She was always writing. She had a voracious intelligence and had graduated with honors from Vassar. Lisa could always be found hunched over her typewriter, pounding out something she would not let anyone read. Lisa had always been able to write. It was her one talent. No one except Kate and her literary agent knew she had just submitted a manuscript for a novel, and she was already at work on a second one. Kate had read the manuscript and hurt, physically, to see how much Lisa was growing as a writer.

The two had met when she first went to work as a fill-in reporter for the New York *Daily Sun*. Lisa did research for one of the senior writers as well as for Kate, and for almost no pay, she also wrote everything from birth announcements to obituaries.

Lisa had her own apartment and a comfortable trust fund, but she was lonely. Kate had more invitations to parties than she knew what to do with, but she needed someone to share the rent. They had lived together now for five years.

Lisa was generous with her talent, often staying in and

reading Kate's first drafts while Kate went out. The best part of the five years was what Kate had consumed of Lisa's knowledge—but it had limits. She knew now how to string words together, but there was magic about Lisa's writing that could not be shared, or learned. Kate had gone so far as to riffle through the notebooks Lisa kept from her writers' group, but it was to no avail. Kate was a journeyman writer. Lisa was an artist.

"Have you heard anything about the Palm Beach assignment?" Lisa asked.

"No."

"You would be perfect for that profile of the playground of the rich. Celebrities visit there all the time."

Last winter, Kate had worked on a profile of the president's daughter. She had written it so vividly, with Lisa's help, that her boss, who crabbed at her mercilessly about her spelling, actually complimented her.

Kate loved to write about famous people, but her real goal was to write fiction, as Lisa did. Kate wanted to become rich and notorious for writing steamy blockbuster novels. And when she set her mind on something, that was it. Nobody had more determination than Kate.

It was twelve-fifteen, and the midday social frenzy at Manchester's was at its peak, with every table filled to capacity. Lunch at Manchester's was always a dressing parade. The bar, where those who couldn't get tables waited, was three deep. The regulars lunched and lingered over decaffeinated espresso for as long as they wanted, no matter how many people were waiting.

Kate was supposed to meet Lawrence, her photographer

friend, for lunch. She arrived early just to check out the crowd.

"Hi, sorry I'm late," Lawrence said as he came up to her.

Lawrence was twenty-eight years old and a freelance photographer who had been in the business for over ten years. He had a thick head of wavy brown hair, sharp features, and a trim athletic body. Kate and he had been on-and-off lovers for a year now.

"That's okay," she said, her eyes moving toward the door. It was the appearance of a tall, aristocratic man who looked to be in his late forties that occupied her attention.

"Who's that?"

"Garrison Morton," Lawrence told her.

"I wonder how he got such a good table," she said, making a note.

"Rich, rich, rich," Lawrence said. "His family commands a lot of respect in banking and social circles. He lives in Palm Beach, and he *never* gives interviews, Kate."

Kate watched Garrison Morton fulfill his social obligations by chatting charmingly with each person at his table. Behind the blue-green eyes, Kate was cool as she made her calculations.

James, the waiter who served the front part of the restaurant, came up to take their orders.

"Chicken hash," Kate said.

"The same," Lawrence told him.

Kate knew that Lawrence was in love with her. And he knew she dated other men, because she was not in love with him. He was sexy, but she had too much ambition to get tied down to any man yet.

"Are we all set for dinner tonight?" he asked.

"I can't, Lawrence. I'm sorry. I don't know when my boss

will be back, and he's going to make his decision on who's going to Palm Beach."

"So call him."

"No, I stand a better chance if I'm there. He likes work-aholics," she replied, restless eyes roaming everywhere to see who was to be seen, know what was to be known.

"Well, you can take time off on your birthday, can't you?" He set his drink down on the table.

"Oh, Lawrence, for Christ's sake!" she said, and regretted the irritation in her voice. "We'll have to do it some other night, I'm sorry."

Kate had never known how to handle people gently. They did not matter to her. She had never learned to give explanations.

The Palm Beach assignment burned in her mind, filling her consciousness, leaving no room for anything else. She had to have this job. It would be her first big break. Nothing could come between her and her objectives. Nothing ever had.

"You can take a few hours off, Kate, you work too much anyway," Lawrence said. "Did you forget it was your birthday?"

She hadn't forgotten; it just didn't matter.

"I've made up my mind, I'm going to get this job, and I won't get it by partying." Her shoulders and upper lip went stiff; the nostrils in her nose flared slightly. "I want to achieve some sort of recognition in this world, Lawrence. Achievement is very important to me."

Lawrence extended his hand to Kate, but his fingers came to rest limply on the table instead when she put her hand in her lap. She was grateful he didn't say anything more.

Lawrence had served his purpose. She had met everyone

who was anyone among his friends in the world of photography and photojournalism. She had used up his connections. He had been a good lay, but not so good that she would sacrifice anything for it, like her ambition.

"What's wrong, Kate?"

"I, uh . . . I need to spend some time alone." The words came out as one word "spendsometimealone."

"Time alone?" he repeated. "What the hell are you talking about? We spend two nights a week together, big deal."

"I don't want to hurt you, Lawrence . . ." her tone overstressing an air of innocence. "I'm just not happy."

He watched her face; if he expected an expression of guilt, what he saw instead was a faint smile, as she gazed at Garrison Morton.

"May I have your attention? We are talking about you and me, Kate," Lawrence said angrily. She looked at him.

"Is this because I can't help you with Palm Beach?"

"No."

"Yes, it is."

"I've simply got to find someone to help me."

"You mean you have to find someone to use."

Kate had never seen him this angry.

"Everybody uses everybody, so what?"

"Did you use me?"

"Didn't you use me?" she countered hotly. In her mind, she had lived up to her half of the bargain. She had given him great sex, been interesting and fun.

"Then let's not prolong this conversation over lunch," Lawrence said, and suddenly, he stood up. "Good-bye and good luck. You'll need it, sweetheart!"

Kate stared after him a moment, shocked, then she smiled slightly, shook her head, and began to eat.

Once more she glanced over at Garrison Morton. This time, he was staring at her, too. Their eyes locked. Kate seized the moment and zeroed in on him with her most flirtatious smile. She had to get him in bed, she thought. He would be invaluable in Palm Beach.

———

Manhattan loomed in front of her, tall buildings, too many people, and streets mired in slush. She was in the backseat of a New York taxi, being jounced from side to side as a driver swerved through the heavy traffic. She opened her daily journal. Kate wrote everything down, every day. She had to find out more about Garrison Morton.

Back in her office, Kate pored over an article about Garrison Morton in the August issue of *Esquire*. He was exactly what she needed. In his mid-forties, rich as Croesus, connected up the wazoo. Over the past month, she had done some research on Palm Beach. She knew it would be hard for her to get interviews. From what she had learned, it seemed that for a few glorious months each year—Thanksgiving to Easter—the residents create a small community that once was the way the town used to exist. Palm Beach falls into the category of things governed by a social tradition whose survival depends on the absence of chance. People there refuse to believe that eventually their town will be extinguished by modern life. In Palm Beach, the old guard was increasingly under siege from the not-so-old guard, and the nouveaux riches. Garrison Morton was old guard.

"I hear Palm Beach is warm this time of year," Al Slocum said. He was the *Sun*'s assignments editor and Kate's boss. He was a short man whose arms seemed to hang down to his ankles. He lived and breathed the paper. Ambition was the only language he understood, and he recognized that same fire in Kate Robinson.

Kate stood up and looked at her boss expectantly.

"Pack your things, Kate," his voice boomed.

Kate swallowed and closed her eyes. She was on her way.

CHAPTER 3

$\mathscr{M}$ark had left a prepaid first-class ticket for her at the Pan Am lounge. Christine found a seat amongst the excitement and stir being caused by a rock star entering the room. She sighed with pleasure as she looked at her ticket. This was her first stake in a new future, and it promised her a life in which she need no longer be a prostitute.

"Is that you, Christine?"

"Hello, Edward," Christine said to a gentleman who approached. She immediately recognized him as a customer—a *former* customer.

"You look wonderful. Your first trip to the States?"

"Yes, Palm Beach."

"Ah, well, wait a minute then." He reached into his jacket pocket, jotted something on a piece of notepaper.

"Here's a telephone number and name. If you ever need any help, call it."

"Whose number?"

"It's not mine. It's just in case you need any help. Keep it."

"I'm not going to need any help."

"I hope not, Christine."

He turned and walked away. Christine turned over the card. On it was the name and telephone number of an Alfred Blum.

———

Only when the plane was aloft did Christine allow her imagination to revel in the possibilities that the future with Mark could hold: the jewels, the clothes, the houses . . . the possibility of marriage and children, which meant more to her than anything else. Respectability, a new start in life.

She looked out the window.

She thought of Palm Beach. America's most enduring playground for the rich and famous. She thought of the enchanted evenings ahead with Mark. The elegant occasions, flickering lights and sweet music, wrapping herself in silk and satin. . . . A new place. A new beginning. A new life, where she didn't have a past or a reputation. Everything around her was a dizzying array of possibilities.

———

"Is that all?" asked the porter at the Palm Beach airport. "You need a taxi?"

"I'm not sure," she replied. "I want to wait just a few more minutes."

Christine stared around her at the strangers in the unfamiliar airport. She began to feel a sinking dread in the pit of her stomach.

"Don't be silly," she said to herself, trying to ease her anxiety. Mark had said if he couldn't make it to the airport, he would meet her at the Airport Hilton.

———

Christine stood in the lobby next to her seven suitcases and two trunks. She wore a rumpled dark blue suit with a white silk blouse, beautifully tailored, suggesting an air of formal elegance. She stood straight, and her manner was severely dignified, just a shade too dignified.

"Mark Althorp's room, please," she said to the desk clerk. She watched the man check and recheck his reservations.

"We have no one by that name. I'm sorry, could it be under another name?"

A slight panic started to fill her.

"Try Christine Wells, please."

"Oh, yes, Miss Wells . . . we have a message for you," he said, handing her an envelope.

Dear Christine,

Unfortunately, sometimes circumstances change, and not always at the most convenient time. I regret that I was unable to reach you prior to your departure from London, because it could have saved you a long and tiring trip.

I have decided, for personal reasons I cannot share with you, not to pursue our relationship any further.

I do wish you the very best, and hopefully one day
you will find what it is you are looking for.

Best,
Mark

It was as though a light had been turned out inside her.

Stunned by the suddenness of the news, and the incompleteness of it all, she could not yet cry, although the room was spinning. Her face was drained of color and her limbs began to tremble.

"Are you all right, ma'am?"

"I'm fine," she said so fast that the man blinked and stepped back.

"May I see your phone book?" There was no Mark Althorp listed.

All at once she began to cry. She was a stranger, in a strange country.

"Oh my God . . ."

"Ma'am?"

She stared blank-eyed at the clerk. Maybe Mark would show up anyway . . . maybe he would change his mind.

Christine came back to reality with a start. She should have listened to Simone. How could she have ever thought she could have a life with him? She was nothing more than a whore.

"I need a room. *Now* please."

While she stood waiting for her key, she felt every pair of eyes in the lobby on her. She wondered whether or not she could make it through the next few minutes without either passing out or getting hysterical.

She followed the bellman into the elevator and then into a small room. She felt a combination of claustrophobia and nausea. She walked to the window. Outside it was dark and depressing. The rain was pouring down.

"Anything else?"

"No, that will be all," she replied, pressing a few dollars into his hand.

Later she lay awake, analyzing again and again how she had misread Mark. She was aware of every noise. She could detect other people's smells on her blanket. She could hear people talking in the next room. She could see a little bit of the dark sky.

She tried to close off her mind and get some sleep. It was impossible. Memories of happy times came flooding in. She was sad and despairing. She had no one. The weather augmented her mood. There was only rain and more rain, and grayness.

The next morning she began to assess her options.

She could go back to London and work for Simone. She could find herself another wealthy man. She could wire the money from her London bank to Palm Beach and start a proper life, erase her past. But how?

She showered, dressed, and ate a solitary meal in the hotel dining room instead of a solitary meal in her solitary room. She glanced around at her fellow guests: There was a young girl with her face buried in a Florida guidebook, an elderly couple, and another lady dining alone. She sat back, running her hands wearily through her hair. The food was not edible, the ambience worse. What was she going to do?

Back in her room, Christine opened one of her old Louis Vuitton trunks filled with her treasures: old bits of tapestries, peacock feathers, silver candlesticks, clocks. A treasure chest . . .

When she was young, she would go to the attic, open her mother's old trunk, and pull out old dresses, blue and lavender hats with exuberant plumes to the crown, purses, everything she needed to create a new image. She used to put the costumes on right over her clothes. The transformation was immediate. She was no longer an ordinary girl. She became special.

That's it, she thought, snapping back to the present. I love fabrics, furniture, candlelight, flowers . . . decorating. She had a knowledge of antiques taught by Simone, and an eye for a bargain. I'll open a small hotel like Simone's, she decided, but without the girls. It will be a legitimate operation.

Despair seemed to drive her inspiration and she was flooded with ideas: where to get financing, style of decor, what kind of building to look for—even the type of paintings on the walls was clear to her. She wrote down her ideas immediately or she knew she would forget them as fresh ones crowded out old ones. The agonizing work for her had always been to develop the idea into reality. Never was that more true than now, but she'd find a way; she had to.

Christine unpacked her treasures, and as she spread them out on the bed and stared at them, a wonderful sense of peace came over her, a sense of peace and purpose.

———

She checked herself into a junior suite in a small hotel off Worth Avenue. The room was really a bedroom and a sitting room in one, not giving her much space, but it was better than that dreadful cubicle at the airport hotel. She had had money wired from London, and for a while at least, she was all right financially.

Over the past few weeks, she had moved in a whirl of nervous energy, a machine that functioned but did not feel. She did not sleep for more than three hours a night because she could not permit herself to sleep—she had too many problems, and not much time.

Christine had made a few inquiries and learned that she definitely could not afford any property on the island of Palm Beach; it would have to be West Palm. The distinction was important, she knew. Old guard and really important people lived in Palm Beach. Everyone else lived across one of three bridges in West Palm. And the towns were separated by more than bridges. Attitudes, class, and status separated them as well—all of this Christine had learned in a very short time.

Knowing she couldn't compete with the grand hotels of Palm Beach and their clients, the idea of a hotel with celebrities in mind was born. Film stars needed somewhere to stay, something a little offbeat, discreet. A place where they could have their privacy in an original setting.

After weeks of looking, that very morning she had seen a rundown old boardinghouse on Clematis Street that she knew had the potential to be a first-class hotel.

She went over the numbers. She could afford the building, but how could she renovate it? The quality of each room would have to be the same standard, as if it were her own home, in order to attract the clientele she desired. She would need a partner. On impulse, she opened the drawer and pulled out the business card with Alfred Blum's name on it. She had to start somewhere; still, she hesitated, and then put the card back without calling him. Someone who knew one of her former clients would have preconceived ideas about her, and she didn't want that. She wanted to start fresh, clean, new.

But necessity dictated otherwise.

She stood before him, too small, too thin for her clothes. The short black skirt flared out from the slim band of her waist. Her blonde hair was gathered carelessly at the back of her neck. She looked very pretty, but tired.

And she was, from days and nights of figuring out how to afford to buy the rooming house and put it in order to attract the best and the wealthiest. And from days and nights of trying to avoid calling Alfred Blum. Any friend of a former client would immediately expect payment in kind. And Christine truly wanted to put that life behind her, start fresh. She was proud of herself for figuring out a way to stay in America, proud of herself for drawing up a legitimate business plan. But she knew that no bank would underwrite her; she had no collateral, no credit. She had been a whore; one of the best and most highly paid, but hardly a recommendation for a bank loan.

So she had called the number on the card, and Alfred Blum agreed to meet her in his offices. He was, he explained, an importer and exporter, a real estate man, an antiques expert—a man of many tastes and abilities. Christine knew without being told that he was also a man of great wealth—just as she knew without being told that he had uncovered her past in London.

She watched him now as he read her proposal. He was an ugly man, enormous both in height and girth. He was in his mid-fifties with thinning dark hair combed straight back from a high forehead and thick lips that chewed a cigar slowly, obscenely. Dark eyes, small and set too close together, blazed with sly intelligence. There was something evil and powerful and strangely sexy about him, despite his lack of good looks.

As he read, Christine hardly breathed. She was both nervous and excited: nervous that he would not like her proposal and then what would she do; excited if he did like it because then what would he want her to do?

"I'm prepared to finance you—" he began.

The words hovered in the air between them.

"And in return?" she prompted.

"That you be profitable within five years," he said, then smiled thinly, "and that you be available to me between four and six times a year, at my command."

"No!" Christine gasped. "I wanted to start a new life. I'm finished with that."

Blum said nothing, just continued to look at her with that thin, knowing smile and that powerful slyness in his eyes.

She stared back at him defiantly, but it was a hollow gesture. She knew that without his help, she was lost. Her choices were limited to returning to London and her life as a whore there, or staying in Palm Beach and becoming a whore here. Better to be one man's whore, she decided, a few times a year, than any man's at any time.

"All right," she whispered.

"I thought you would see it my way," he said, nodding complacently. "I will be in touch soon to finalize the details."

Christine thought she would hear from him the next day, and she did, by way of a brief but formal note confirming their business arrangement: A sum of one million dollars had been placed in an account for her at the Florida National Bank. He was her silent partner in the new hotel venture, named not yet determined, and for that million dollars, he was to receive 65 percent of all profits when the venture began to earn a profit—plus the pleasurable services of the owner for a minimum of four times a year.

She signed the agreement, the heaviness in her heart lessened only by the knowledge that even with the strings attached, Palm Beach and the hotel *were* a new start for her.

———

Christine bought the old boardinghouse, and over the next few months, an army of workmen converted the upstairs into lavish suites. Room by room, she set about restoring, renovating, and decorating. If she had any problems, she mentioned Mr. Blum; it brought an immediate change in attitude.

The lobby was done in inky blue walls and floors, with swathes of gray silk curtains.

One entire floor was done in black. Another in dark green.

"Put on three coats of emulsion and then polyurethane, so it doesn't show the dirt," Christine instructed the painter. She believed a coat of dark paint could transform anything.

"The lighting is very important. I do not want to be affected by the sun or the clouds. I want to create my own mood," she explained to the electrician, sitting comfortably in a chair in her suite of rooms on the fourth floor.

She had finished off her personal suite early so she could live on the premises to supervise. There were black silk taffeta curtains, lined thickly; a four-poster bed draped in black taffeta; an armoire inlaid with mother-of-pearl; and a round table next to the bed with a cut-glass bowl of gardenias. An air of dreamlike luxury pervaded.

Her last six months had been well spent. There were many twenty-hour days but she was thankful for them. Her work had stopped her from thinking of Mark. He symbolized all she had lost: the possible marriage, the love, the family. Instead, she was becoming a businesswoman. And the two times Alfred had "demanded" her company had been less unpleasant than she had anticipated. He was a considerate lover and an adept one. Other than those two occasions, Christine had not been with a man since coming to Palm Beach. There was time enough for that later.

A few days before the grand opening, Christine stood in the lobby wearing black tights and an oversized black T-shirt. She had on a black padre hat, reminiscent of those worn by priests in Italy. The hat looked like a black halo hovering over her light blonde hair.

The hotel radiated with Christine's energy; her movements filled the rooms with eloquent commotion. Each room seemed a trophy to her passion for her project.

Christine was doing another one of her walk-throughs. She was, as always, immersed in a myriad of conversations, none of which she ever completed: She talked to an elderly gentleman about the linens; she walked over to a seamstress and argued about the length of the draperies; she yelled at a workman about dripping paint on a carpet. The more agitated she was, the higher her voice rose, until at times, she reached high soprano.

She turned the key to the last suite to be completed on the sixth floor. A rush of fresh, spring potpourri sweetened the air.

All of the bedrooms were formal, intimate, and unique, with such accoutrements as antique steamer trunks, old black telephones, and gilded bird cages. She had even forfeited some of the precious silk Chinese rugs given to her by a former "client," and brought in some of her own candlesticks too.

Christine was a perfectionist; no detail was too miniscule

to warrant her attention. She was dictatorial and difficult about how everything was combined, but the results were extraordinary.

With a trembling hand, she made some final notes to herself. She glanced at her watch. It was time to go to the airport. The past two weeks she had been spending three hours a night there, tipping taxi drivers so they would bring guests who might not have made prior arrangements to her hotel.

She leaned over to center a beaten brass bowl full of shimmering lilies on a table in the hallway. When she straightened, she looked at herself in the mirror above.

"I'm ready," she whispered under her breath, her nerves as thin and brittle as a wafer.

CHAPTER 4

*A*n invitation to the opening of Seasons had been sent to Kate at the Colony Hotel. All of the press had been invited.

"I hear everyone who is anyone will be there," she said on the phone to her boss, Al Slocum. "Normally, the opening of another hotel wouldn't draw the Palm Beachers, but everyone knows Alfred Blum is the backer, and there is a certain curiosity value surrounding him."

"There should be," Slocum laughed. "The rumor is he deals in illegal arms. . . . You've got to get him to talk, Kate, no matter what you have to do," he said, the implication

clear. Another woman might have been unsuited to this—
but Kate was a pro, a hard-nosed journalist who was proud
of her ability to maneuver people any way she could to get
her story.

She had been in town for three weeks now, her second
trip to Palm Beach a gift from Al because she had done so
well in her earlier assignment. She was staying at the Colony
Hotel, a British colonial-inspired Palm Beach landmark, famous for its celebrated clientele, its lively bar activity, and
dancing. It was perfect for her, conveniently located one
block from Worth Avenue, and one block from the Atlantic
Ocean where she could work on her tan, ensuring she looked
great.

So far, she had had no luck meeting Garrison Morton. His
secretary always said he was out of town. Kate had been
keeping herself busy researching Alfred Blum. He was a
mystery in town. Society had ignored him until he had appeared on the *Forbes* annual list of the four hundred richest
people in America. The very people who once would not
invite him to their parties became the first to invite him now.

Kate leafed through her notes. Blum had come from nowhere, too, and had accumulated one of the greatest fortunes
in America in record time, but from what, no one was quite
sure. He was a frequent visitor to the White House and had
achieved social and business success in Palm Beach without
benefit of inheritance or heritage, because of the grand sums
of money he donated to the social advancement charities or
the old-guard charities, as they are called, such as the Pres-
ervation Society, Planned Parenthood, and the Red Cross.

Kate had driven past the Blum estate several times, which
stretched from the ocean to the lake on the south end of the
island. From the road, one could see nothing of the house

and gardens, hidden behind the 30-foot-high hedges that surrounded the property. The only visible structures were the greenhouses, where, Kate had learned, Mrs. Blum grew her orchids, and the kennels, which housed the police dogs that patrolled the grounds at night.

Mrs. Blum was also a mystery. She very rarely accompanied her husband to the gala events his wealth required him to attend. Rumor had it she drank a lot. Oddly, Blum remained scrupulously faithful—at least in public. And the lack of any information on him made Kate even thirstier.

After Kate hung up with her boss, she decided to try Morton again.

"Mr. Morton, please."

"Who's calling?"

"Kate Robinson."

"Will Mr. Morton know what this is in reference to?" asked the woman.

"I am doing a piece on Palm Beach for *Vanity Fair,* and I would like a few minutes of Mr. Morton's time," she lied.

"Mr. Morton is extremely busy."

"Well, you could let Mr. Morton decide whether or not he is too busy. Isn't it his decision?" she asked irritably. Kate hated secretaries.

There was an icy silence.

"Just a moment."

Kate pictured an imperious, pale-skinned little woman on the other end of the line.

"I'm sorry . . . Mr. Morton is busy. Good-bye, Miss Robinson."

Kate pressed her lips together, making her mouth one blade-thin line.

Frustrated, she threw her pencil down. She would have to

find another path to these people. She desperately needed a social connection for her professional life. Perhaps she'd find that someone tonight.

———

The cars rolled slowly up to the front entrance of Seasons: a fleet of Bentleys, Rolls-Royces, Jaguars, and Mercedes. Strobe lights flashed and the blinding lights of local television cameras were going off as recognizable Palm Beach society entered the hotel.

Kate gave her rental car to the valet, and walked up the path to the hotel. In the front hallway, a woman handed her a pen to sign the guest book. Her eyes scanned the signatures. She recognized many of the illustrious names.

She wandered into a reception salon, her eyes darting everywhere. The room was packed with bodies and faces, so tightly that one could not distinguish at a glance which faces belonged to which bodies; she decided to make a rapid tour inspection of the other rooms.

There were two dining rooms, where there were tables for ten with beautiful fresh orchids as centerpieces on pink moiré tablecloths. Buffet tables were set up with crystal, china, and silver, all bearing the letter *S*. There was a sumptuous cold buffet selection of Scottish salmon, Maine lobster, and Florida bay prawns, and a hot entree selection of swordfish steaks, and boned quail stuffed with foie gras. There was also a conference room that had been turned into a fairyland of flower arrangements and twinkling lights for dancing later, and a library.

Waiters carried trays with Pol Roger 1975 vintage pink champagne from one room to the other, which necessitated a circuitous routing. Not knowing where to station herself to full advantage to witness the evening, Kate decided on a position at the foot of the staircase, where she would not miss a single entrance into the main reception area, and she could clearly see one dining room.

"Old money, old money," one woman was saying to another, kissing her on both cheeks.

"Married four times, sleeps with everybody."

"Really," replied the small woman with a big head, topped by a Brigitte Bardot hairstyle. She abandoned the other woman in midsentence and darted in the direction of the patio, obviously having spotted someone more important.

Kate spotted Reginald Pearce standing near the fireplace. She recognized him from a piece she had read in *Town and Country* about him and his role as lynchpin in Palm Beach, "America's most enduring playground for the rich and famous." According to the magazine, he represented a facade of strength, confidence, and status based on heritage and ancestry.

As she looked around, Kate recalled the introduction to her own first article on the area. She had described Palm Beach as an unique bastion of power and money, a capital of affluence, where the median age was sixty-three. It was home to retired heads of industry, to statesmen, and to financiers. Many of its families were tied into generational money, funds passed down for as long as several hundred years. They were the old guard: old money, old name, the bluebloods with their proper education, breeding, and backgrounds; the ones not easy to reach out and touch. To Kate, they were tantalizingly impenetrable. Even tonight, their greetings were like a New York fall day, crisp and cool.

"I wonder where Ms. Wells comes from," someone whispered behind Kate. "Ancestry is priceless, you know, and can't be bought or earned, or even decorated tastefully, much as one might try."

Reginald was talking to his fourth wife, Gladys Pearce, who was also from a good old family, impeccably dressed tonight in unpretentious white satin. Kate knew she headed up the Garden Club and the Wextal Art Gallery, two very exclusive society establishments. In Palm Beach, the clubs and restaurants and shops that kept the privileged in and the riffraff out were what mattered. Reginald and Gladys were revered here in the manner that the very rich are revered in America—not for their character, but for their breeding and bank accounts. Kate was jealous of the silver platter that life had handed them.

On the opposite side of the spectrum were the nouveaux riches: the status seekers, big supporters of charity, the ones Kate had no trouble talking to—they loved the press— which is why the lack of information about Alfred Blum was so tantalizing.

Kate had read back issues of *Palm Beach Life* magazine, *Palm Beach Society,* and the local *Palm Beach Daily News*—the Shiny Sheet. She recognized many of the faces this evening.

She hadn't needed a magazine to recognize Garrison Morton, though. As he entered the hotel, without a date Kate was pleased to see, she vowed she would get to know him. He was too handsome and too rich; she *had* to have him.

Morton was talking with a group of four or five men, men Kate had taken to privately labeling "the bachelors." They sat nightly at someone's home balancing out tables where there were widows or divorced ladies of quality. She also spotted various members of deposed royal families of Yugoslavia and Romania.

Cornelia Mason advanced into the hotel in tiny little running steps, her left hand clutching her breast beneath her grape-sized pearls, her other hand fluttering at her right side. She had just returned from Paul Niehans clinic at Vevey, Switzerland, for her annual rejuvenating treatment. Kate had read a scathing article on the aging widow of the auto tycoon, and Cornelia had been furious, because they had made fun that her dogs had a daily printed menu. No one made fun of her dogs.

Kate watched as everyone broke up into their own subgroups. The royals were at one table, the old guard at another, the new people in town, whose wealth was incalculable, at another.

Eventually, Alfred Blum entered the room. Kate stared at him, fascinated. He was unhandsome and compelling at the same time. He had on black-framed, dark-lensed glasses, which he never removed.

A waiter raced to serve him champagne. His massiveness filled the doorway. He took his handkerchief from his breast pocket and wiped lipstick off his cheek. Blum's presence possessed a kind of power that made ordinary conversation seem trite.

His wife stood next to him—her rare appearance underscoring the truth to the rumors that Blum had a vested interest in tonight's success. She looked remote, elegant, and sad as his counterweight.

Kate pressed her way forward.

Alfred shook Kate's hand in passing, met her eyes, and sized her up in an instant as someone whom he had very little interest in—she wasn't a well-enough-known writer. It was a greeting of an important host to an unimportant guest. Kate read all this immediately, and silently vowed that someday *soon* this kind of attitude would change.

She watched him take a seat at a table. Then she helped herself to the cold buffet and found an empty seat at the table next to his.

At her dinner table, everyone was engaged in animated conversation. There was a darkly handsome man, his tan obviously artificial, who bought and sold estate jewelry. There was a very well known art dealer; at his right was the daughter of a copper mining mogul. She spoke in the friendly but distant manner that wealthy women possess, a manner that assumed everyone knew exactly who she was. She lit cigarettes throughout the entire meal. On her left was a count who was now a real estate salesman at Sotheby's. Kate wondered if it was a bogus title.

Next to him was another heiress, who was married to an opera star, absent this evening. She was blazing with huge emeralds and Kate didn't know whether to look at her emeralds or her protruding teeth.

One seat away from Kate was a New York millionairess who was now seeking Palm Beach recognition. She was in a garish creation of violet-colored lamé with a silver brocade bodice. Jewels glittered at neck and wrist.

"What do you do?" she asked Kate.

"I'm a reporter for a New York paper covering the Palm Beach social scene."

"Are you the one who wrote about Cornelia Mason?" Her mouth moved into an upturned crescent. It resembled a smile.

"No."

"What are you writing about?"

"Oh, a little of this, a little of that," Kate replied, shrugging, dismissing the subject as either too unimportant or too mysterious to discuss.

Kate listened, as she always did, to three or four conversations at a time. She gave them her full attention, whether they were witty or dull, intriguing or boring. Someday all this might come in handy—in a book about these people. There was little the residents of Palm Beach didn't know about each other, and very little they didn't discuss. Tonight she was finding out who was old rich, who was nouveau, who took drugs, who had problems with alcohol, who was sleeping with whom, who was straight and who was gay. During her first trip, she had hustled for interviews with visiting celebrities. This time she wanted to learn about the natives, hopefully to convince Al that the paper should have a full-time columnist based here. Kate had fallen in love with Palm Beach. It had everything she wanted from life: money, money, money. And people with power. This evening's affair was a gossip writer's dream, with so many of Palm Beach's most influential people gathered in one place. There were connections to be made, and more important, knowledge to be learned.

One thing she was learning was what the people thought of Seasons. The beauty of the hotel, the tastefulness of the decor, were discussed with varying degrees of approval. What people considered far more interesting was Alfred Blum's backing—by now commonly acknowledged as true —and the connection between him and the beautiful, mysterious owner who was circulating now among her guests.

Kate had heard little tidbits of gossip about her: She was said to be British; she had simply arrived in Palm Beach one day and the next thing anyone heard was that Alfred Blum was financing her purchase and renovation of the old hotel. Seeing the lovely young woman, Kate had no doubt there was more to the relationship than business, but neither

Christine Wells nor Alfred Blum did anything more compromising than occasionally nod at each other throughout dinner. Kate was sure there was something deliciously sinful about Christine Wells's past. No one simply appeared in Palm Beach without some sort of secret or story they wished to keep hidden; not even the super-rich were immune. It would be fun, Kate decided, to stick around long enough to find out exactly what Christine Wells was all about.

After dinner, some people went into the courtyard for liqueurs while others went into the room that had been set up for dancing. That became Kate's destination when she saw Garrison Morton go in there. She spotted him standing against one wall, chatting with another man, and she maneuvered her way through the crowd over to him. His warm smile, the easy shrug of his shoulders seemed to say that nothing weighed too much within his soul.

Kate was trying to find the right moment to approach him when the music changed to a very slow tune.

"Do you dance?" she asked in her most sexy tone.

He stopped in midconversation to look at the stranger. Obviously he was pleased with what he saw because he didn't ignore her. Kate was grateful for that.

"I'm a lousy dancer," he said.

"Well, I never believe a man who uses that excuse," Kate said, taking him by the hand and leading him to the dance floor. "Are you enjoying yourself?"

"Not particularly," said Garrison. "However, I'm a friend of Alfred's."

"By the way . . . my name is Kate Robinson."

"Garrison Morton," he replied hesitantly. "I understand you called me this afternoon."

"I did."

"What for?"

"I just wanted to talk to you for a few minutes over lunch or something. . . . I'm a journalist from New York covering the Palm Beach scene and I think you'd be an interesting subject."

"Well . . . I'll think about it, but I'm leaving for Cat Cay tomorrow to do some fishing. Maybe sometime next week," Garrison told her. "Call my secretary," he suggested.

Kate laughed. "I've had a lot of success with her the past few weeks."

"I presume about as much success as I'm going to have finding your boss at *Vanity Fair.*"

Garrison looked at her face. There was no tension or guilt, only radiant mockery—the look of dangerously unpredictable amusement.

Kate moved into him, putting her cheek to his comfortably.

————

Christine was happy as her guests wandered from room to room, music playing in the background.

She was dressed in a simple and elegant black velvet sheath. Her blonde hair was parted in the middle, held back by two Cartier barrettes.

Alfred's secretary had handled the guest list, and almost everyone showed up. Tonight was a glorious success, and the small price Alfred exacted for his help now seemed well worth it.

Suddenly, the appearance in the lobby of a tall, handsome gentleman occupied all of Christine's attention. At his side was a woman with yellow diamonds in great quantity at her ears and neck. Her brown hair was combed straight back and

coiled silkily in a bun at the nape of her neck. She stood
regally tall, her chin lifted.

The man edged his way into the room, murmuring greetings to certain people, smiling smugly.

Christine blanched.

He made the gesture of kissing Mrs. Blum's hand, then he
chatted a moment with Alfred.

Christine stood for several minutes staring at him; finally
their eyes met. He looked straight at her. There was absolutely nothing there: no anger, no sadness, no love, no hate.
Mark Althorp's eyes were empty. He made her feel as if she
did not exist.

He remained with his wife. He laughed with her, appearing the attentive, devoted, admiring husband. In that
instant, Christine saw what a weak, pitiful wish she had
nurtured. She had been a fool. The truth was staring her
in the face—she would always be a prostitute. She shut
her eyes tightly not wanting to see reality. Her heart was
pounding.

She walked unsteadily from the room, fearing that she
was going to be sick or faint, and went upstairs to her private
suite. She needed to be alone to regain her composure so
that no one—not Alfred, not the rich and powerful of Palm
Beach—could know how she felt. It was important to maintain the facade of cool, calm poise. She was a businesswoman
now, and if Seasons was really to take off, her reputation as
a competent woman would be vitally important.

She went into the luxurious bathroom off the bedroom to
fix her face, dab ice cold water on the back of her neck. Then
she dried herself with the thick Descamps face towel. Still
feeling faint, she repeated the process. When she walked out,
a woman was standing there.

"I'm Kate Robinson." She offered her hand. "I didn't know anyone was here. I was looking for the powder room."

"This is the private quarters," Christine said coldly. "The guest powder room is downstairs."

What Christine could not possibly have known was that Kate had deliberately followed her. After dancing with Garrison she had left for the ladies' room. That's when she had observed the interplay between the hotel owner and the new arrival, and then Christine's hasty retreat. Kate had quickly put two and two together and come up with the conviction that Christine was one jilted female. Befriending her could be Kate's passport to the rich and famous.

"I'm sorry, I didn't know," Kate said, starting toward the door as if she were heading out.

Christine sighed, and looked down at the plush carpeting as if the other woman wasn't there.

"It doesn't matter," she murmured.

Kate came back into the room and stood near her. "Are you all right?"

Christine glanced up and into the warm, compassionate facade of Kate Robinson. "I'm Christine Wells. What did you say your name was?"

Kate told her.

"I didn't mean to be rude to you before," Christine said. "It's just that—"

"I know, you and—"

"Mark. I guess you could tell that he and I . . ."

"Christine, his name is not Mark."

Christine stared at Kate open-mouthed, her eyes growing large and unnaturally bright, but this time, not with unshed tears. This time, what she felt was unmitigated shock.

CHAPTER 5

QUEEN OF SPADES: *Ruled by work and the quest for wisdom*

*J*essie Malcolm went over to the kitchen cabinet. She rummaged around and pulled out a box of Duncan Hines Brownie Mix.

Allison was crouched on the green sofa watching Bugs Bunny run away from an angry cartoon man. She had sucked all the juice out of her thumb; it was wrinkled and milk-white.

"I feel like making brownies. What wants to help me? Who's gonna lick the bowl?" There were smiles in Jessie's voice.

"Me, me," squealed the three-year-old, her blonde curls

bouncing as she ran to her mother, a grin spreading across her face.

They kissed. Foreheads. Cheeks. Lips. Butterflies with their eyelashes. Everything on their faces was brushed by the other's kisses.

The afternoon was muggy. The humidity and Jessie's long brown hair were fighting it out in her un-air-conditioned house. Her fingers tugged haphazardly through the tight web of curls, trying to make the recalcitrant hair obey her. She wore no makeup, yet she was a radiantly lovely twenty-two. She opened the window higher for more air.

Jessie was tall, five feet ten inches tall, with long, firm, show-girl legs. She was diet thin, but she had to work at it. She walked with a masculine, straight-line abruptness, yet she had a peculiar grace of motion that was swift, and challengingly feminine. Her extraordinary mane of long chestnut-brown hair touched the lines of her shoulder blades. Her thick brows rose in two straight wings, giving her a strangely insolent air, and a thick fringe of dark brown lashes dominated her small, beautiful face.

A faint dusting of freckles ran across the bridge of her small nose. And her wide, vulnerable mouth drooped slightly at the corners, as though she were a little sad. She had enormous aquamarine blue eyes. In the planes of her face, there was a proud purity.

Chicken juices hissed and bubbled in the kitchen, but Jessie's mind wasn't on the dinner; it was on her husband. And her marriage.

Jessie and Jake had started dating each other at age sixteen. There had been no other men in her life. She did not know whether this made her unhappy. She had no time to know. Jessie had gotten pregnant in her senior year and dropped out of school. Jake had graduated, and immediately went to work for Southern Bell, where he still continued to make a meager living. They lived in a small, rundown, two-bedroom Spanish-style house in downtown West Palm Beach.

Jessie looked out the window at the trail of pink and white impatiens that led to the sidewalk. Her left hand was on the kitchen faucet. She saw the rays come off her engagement ring. Where had things gone wrong? There had never been any talk of love, but there had always been a comfortable warmth between them. Now, even that was gone.

For months, she had been trying to resolve the many problem areas in her mind. In the early married years, her life was a numbing blur of pizza and beer-drinking parties. Next, it had aggravated him that she wouldn't smoke pot. It made a gap between them. Her high energy was annoying to his mellowness. Now he was constantly making digs at her fervent quest for information, knowledge. Her eyes welled up. What she felt wasn't pain or grief—just regret for not being able to make things work. It gripped her like a steel claw.

"Are they ready, Mommy?"

"Here you go, my angel. . . . Be careful, they're warm," she said, forcing the sadness from her eyes.

Jessie watched her daughter eat. Could she ever do to her daughter what had been done to her?

Would she ever be able to divorce Jake and have him be just a visitor? There are gifts that only a father can give a daughter: his gentle presence, his daily reassuring, his solemn declaration to always protect her. Jessie had been robbed of those gifts. Could she rob her daughter of them too?

"Daddy's home," Allison squealed, rushing toward the front door, throwing herself into Jake's chest.

"Hey, how's my princess?"

"Mommy and I made brownies!"

"Oh boy! And have you been a good girl today?"

"Yep," Allison replied, nodding her head vigorously.

"Hi Jessie," his voice was louder when he spoke to her. It always sounded as if he were trying hard at something. "How was your day?" He looked at her, scanning every inch of her body.

She was dressed in cut-off jeans and a white tank top. She stood as she always did, straight and lean. She had an electric, effortless sexuality that was painful to him because he never seemed able to unleash it.

"I'm fine." Her teeth were very white against her suntanned face.

"Dinner will be ready at six." She handed Jake a beer, their hands not touching.

Who is this man? Jessie wondered, not for the first time. Jake was tall and lithe, with sinewy muscles and strong thighs, but his face was out of focus, a mystery to her.

Jessie studied his smooth face, his full lips, until they became less strange to her. Yes, I used to know that face. When did things go wrong?

"I started a painting this afternoon while Allison was sleeping. You want to see it?"

"Yeah, great," he responded. The tone did not match the meaning of the word. She knew he blamed Maria, her psychic friend, for her interest in art. She had told Jessie she had significant potential as a painter. He hated all that rubbish. But Maria was important to her—she provided a form of nurturing Jessie had lost many years ago.

Jake had no interest to spare for her hobbies or interests. He had his basketball and his beer-drinking buddies. He was singularly unencumbered in his mind.

Jessie could no longer disguise from herself the boredom she felt with Jake. It crept over her with cruel force. She had done her best to struggle against it, but for months now, she had been suffering from terrible insomnia. Painting, her one passion, had even become wearisome. Her own paintings seemed tepid to her, reflecting, as they did, her flattened-out emotions. She summoned all her willpower to beat back the insidious erosion that threatened her marriage. Her art and her life felt stuck in the present with its shrunken possibilities and broken promises. Allison was her only source of joy.

She puzzled in vain over answers that never would arrange themselves in any sort of finale. Where was she going?

"Do you want anything else?"

"Nope."

"How was your day?"

"Fine."

As usual, the dinner conversation was uncomfortable, and boring.

"I think I'll see if they need any part-time help at the art gallery."

"You know how I feel about you working, Jessie. Your place is at home with Allison."

"She's in day care, Jake. You told me to wait until she was old enough, then you promised me I could go to work. I need something else in my life . . . to nourish myself, Jake."

He stared blankly.

"What is love to you, Jake?" she asked. She looked straight into his eyes, her own wide and questioning, and guileless.

"Don't start this again, Jessie."

"What is love?" she insisted.

"It's too difficult and complex to describe."

"No, Jake, it is exquisite and simple . . . extend yourself to nourish another."

"You should be happy with what I've provided for you." His voice was cold.

"There is no possibility of happiness for me, Jake, if it is based on *your* list of happiness."

This happened frequently now. She questioned Jake. He listened to her, answered some questions, but Jessie felt that she was knocking against a sheet of iron in Jake's unmoving eyes, and that they were not speaking about the same things at all.

They sat silently, searching desperately for a road that would lead them back to where they had been. Yet Jessie knew. For months now she had known. She had been resolving things in her mind, but had not been able to resolve them in her heart.

Jessie finished tucking Allison in, then went into her room. She wondered why she always felt it at this time of day, this sense of dread. Had she always felt it? No, she hadn't, but she couldn't remember when it started. She thought of her childhood. She loved its memories, at least the early part of it; she wished a few rays from that time could reach her present. She remembered a summer day when she was eight years old. That day, at the beach, her father was telling her what she should do. The words were glowing, like sunlight. Jessie had listened in admiration and wonder.

"You must always reach for the best within yourself," he had said.

She had never learned how people could want to do otherwise; she had learned only that they did.

Jessie sighed, then started to cry, because she knew she had to leave Jake. Divorce? A legion of demons suddenly appeared at her back. . . .

She was twelve years old, sitting on the front steps on Almeria Street in downtown West Palm Beach, waiting for her father to come and take her for the weekend. She couldn't remember when this waiting for her father began. Was she ten, or even younger? All she knew was that it became a weekend ritual, something she could set her clock and heart on. Weekdays, Mommy. Weekends, Daddy. How come? she would ask. That was the way it was, her mother explained over and over. It made sense to the adults, but to Jessie it was lonely and lopsided. Why didn't Mommy and Daddy and I all live together? she often wondered.

In Jessie's mind, their tiny clapboard house wasn't big enough to hold her father's beauty. Everywhere he walked, the rooms seemed to light up. Such elegance belonged on a Hollywood screen, not in an ordinary living room, on an ordinary street, in ordinary West Palm Beach.

When was he coming? When? He never missed one of his weekends, and he was always around for the special occasions that punctuated her childhood. She never had to ask him; he always showed up. He would sit in the front row watching her perform her tap dance on stage. He beamed as she sang her heart out at the school play or pirouetted across the stage. His applause was always the loudest, his smile the brightest. He reassured her that her church recital dress was beautiful; that *she* was beautiful. Her heart stopped at the sight of the dark blue Chevrolet. She heard the horn. It was her father.

"Daddy!" She let out a little scream, rushing toward the car.

Her father was tall and slender. His nails were always polished and buffed, his wavy brown hair always immaculately combed. Jessie was so dazzled, she couldn't speak. He seemed to glide up the sidewalk with his brilliant smile.

"How's Daddy's girl?" He bent down, grabbing her up in a ferocious squeeze and she breathed in his Old Spice. It was strong and it made her dizzy. Her face snuggled into his cheek, happy to be with him, already dreading the moment when he would have to go.

"Okay, Jessie, let's see what you can do."

He pulled a baseball out from the backseat and two gloves. Another ritual. *Their* ritual. They threw twenty, thirty, forty good clean catches back and forth on the street, in front of the house, one right after the other.

Jessie had small wet circles underneath her arms, and drops were beading on her forehead and dripping down from her hairline. She would rather die than have it be over.

They were laughing as they threw the ball. Sweating, laughing, having a good time. The sound of her father's laughter bounced from her ears into her soul. . . .

Too soon the weekend was over and it was time for her father to drive her home.

"Jessie, it's time," he would say, standing by the car.

"Not yet," she would cry.

For an instant, her father looked as frozen as a mannequin in Penney's windows.

She ran to him and stood in the circle of his arms, her face hidden against his chest. He looked down at her and stroked her hair.

"Be good."

"I will."

One day, she might have her father all the time again. That was her dream, but until then, she needed a way to fill his absences. She knew she would have to go through a whole week before she saw him again, so, sometimes, to bring him closer, she carried the baseball games around in her head. When she concentrated, she could hear him.

"I love you, baby." His hug captured her breath; his words took hold of her, a strong grip she cherished.

———

Her father's voice seemed so distant now. His tone reverberated against a foggy memory. She grabbed for it, but like a smoke ring, it disappeared. What remained crystal clear was the memory of her stepfather. . . .

Little Miss Barbie Doll went sailing through the air, crashing head first into the base of the bureau. From her standing position in the middle of her double bed, Jessie hurled Ken in the same direction.

"I want Daddy," she sobbed until she felt the room engulf her like the sea. Her shoulders were vibrating up and down. She was drowning.

"What is wrong with you?" her mother asked urgently. "What is it?"

"You don't love me," she hiccupped. "You only love him."

"Jessie," her mother began, "of course I love you."

Jessie knew that her mother believed sensible people cried only about life-threatening situations, such as when there was no food, no money, sickness. It was hard for her to tolerate that her daughter was standing in the middle of the bedroom whining for more love.

"Just because I remarried doesn't mean I don't love you," she said, grasping Jessie's fingers. "And Raymond loves you, too."

Jessie snatched her hand away.

"You need to stop this foolishness, Jessie," her mother said sternly.

"Why did you have to marry him?" Jessie screamed, furious. "I hate him!"

"But he hasn't done anything to you. . . . He loves you."

"No he doesn't."

Jessie didn't look at her. She couldn't. She was too scared.

Could she tell her? Could she tell her Raymond came in when she was in the tub and tried to touch her? Could she ruin her mother's new life?

"When you calm down, come downstairs to say good night to me and your stepfather," her mother said, straining for patience. "And hurry, Jessie. I'm late for work."

She was afraid to look her stepfather in the face, as though he were the sun and would burn out her eyeballs. She kept her distance, mostly looking down at her feet.

Her mother hugged her good-bye before she went to waitress at the diner. The smell of her Emeraude perfume filled Jessie's nostrils. It was sweetly oppressive, and she turned away with a sharp, sudden hunger for her father's Old Spice. It was during the nighttime she needed him the most.

Her life became so sad, and looking back from the advantage of years, Jessie felt that the shift in the memories was as penetrating as the change in perfumes. Once her nighttimes had been enveloped by stories told to her by the man she adulated whose warmth surrounded her and sent her off to dreamland. But the scene shifted and there was Raymond creeping into her bedroom piercing the security of a child's innocent sleep. He had damaged her, that was for sure. But the more she matured, the more she was determined to heal, to open the windows Raymond's abuse had closed for her. Jessie wanted to learn to love for real.

She waited until she knew that Jake would be asleep before going to the bedroom. Lately he'd taken to drinking enough to anesthetize himself, and Jessie couldn't blame him. Sometimes she wanted to do the same. Their life together was a lake so shallow it could not cool in summer. She wanted to get out of it, and yet she feared for Allison. When would she know the answer? Soon, the voice inside her said, soon.

CHAPTER 6

QUEEN OF DIAMONDS:
Ruled by materialism

A blizzard had hit Poughkeepsie, and the Vassar campus was now blanketed in snow. Sarah Potter sat in her BMW warming the engine until Lisa Greene, who was visiting from New York City, finished dressing back in the dorm room. Lisa worked as a researcher for some magazine or newspaper in the city. The two young women had nothing in common except their trust funds, but their families were good friends so Sarah was playing welcome wagon hostess to the mousey writer this weekend.

Sarah adjusted her chestnut-brown hair that was ironing-board straight and pulled back with a black velvet Chanel bow. When she looked in the rearview mirror, she admired what she saw.

Sarah Potter, at eighteen, was imperious and confident, with a chiseled, angular face and a liquid grace in her long, lean body that she carried with the sophistication of one much older. She was an overindulged child who came from money on both sides. Her father had been from a family that had made a fortune in textiles and then the music business. Her mother was from a distinguished New York and Northeast Harbor family. It was a perfect union, smiled on by both sides.

While she was growing up, her father, whom Sarah revered, and who adored and doted on her in return, worked hard. Her mother, whom Sarah thought was dreadful, ignored Sarah. The clubs were all-important to her mother—the clubs in Southampton, Palm Beach, Newport. Sarah had been raised with the words "but darling, they are not eligible for any of the clubs." It was a phrase she had heard all her life. Her mother, in spite of Sarah's feelings toward her, was a most accomplished woman. She rode. She could shoot. She could paint well. She could sculpt. Because of this, her mother was constantly telling Sarah *she* should do something with her life, but Sarah liked to go to parties and listen to music with her headphones. She had changed her major three times. She was not driven to do anything but have a good time.

Sarah was jealous of her mother, who was more beautiful than she was, and she was even more jealous of her parents' relationship with each other. They had meant more to each other than she meant to them. Consequently, she had become a wild child, asked to leave one prep school for cheating on a French exam, and another for using drugs in her room, even after her father had offered to build a new library. Her father had always bailed her out of everything. She was now in her second year at Vassar, majoring in liberal arts.

"Hi," said Lisa, hopping into the passenger seat. "Where are we going?"

"To Patrick's," Sarah said as she pulled away from the medieval-style buildings.

"Who's Patrick?"

"Fun."

Patrick was the campus drug dealer. Sarah was cultivated, yet she enjoyed the contrast, or the punishment, of another lifestyle. She was simply bored dating people who had no more ambition than their next game of squash, backgammon, or bridge. There were many lovers. She was set into a pattern of sexual relationships with people she barely knew. It was a compulsive sexual need to make up for her own void. The men were like a drug to her. She did a lot of stoned sex, sometimes blacking out. It passed for intimacy and made her feel a false connection with people. Her life was a constant commute between two different worlds—half her drive was toward the world of money and status, the other toward men who did nothing and had less. Her addictions were not to drugs or alcohol. They were to more subtle and dangerous things like excitement and danger.

Within minutes, they were parking in front of a house in a less-than-great area of Poughkeepsie. As they neared the front door, which was unlocked, the sound level rose. The two girls stepped inside and were instantly swept into the pulsating beat of the party. Very loud voices mingled with the rhythmic sound of the Eagles blasting from stereo speakers.

At least eighty people were packed inside the rundown old town house near Route 9W. In each corner of the living room a bar had been set up with cans of beer, cheap white wine, and plastic glasses. At that moment, Sarah could have killed for a glass of champagne, but that seemed out of the question in this crowd. Here and there, girls and guys, their leather clothes clearly marking them as members of a motor-cycle gang, tipped back small bottles of hard booze, and the smell of cigarette smoke plus marijuana wafted over the crowd. In the corner of the living room a small group was gathered around a cheap glass coffee table where lines of cocaine were laid out on a mirror. This was how the dealer drummed up business: He gave away freebies once in a while at parties. Sarah had met Patrick, a native of Pough-keepsie, when she had attended his last "Open House." She vaguely remembered having sex with someone in one of the upstairs rooms. She thought he might have kept his black leather jacket on while they were making love, though she wasn't clear on all the details. She only hoped he wasn't here now.

Lisa breathed in the acrid smoke and shivered with dis-taste. She didn't do drugs.

"What do we do now?" she asked Sarah.

"We have a drink," Sarah said, dragging Lisa through the crowd to the bar. Sarah had already had two glasses of champagne back at her dorm room while dressing. She didn't like to walk into a party unless she had a few drinks and a hit of coke, which added to the fun of getting dressed in one of her drop-dead outfits. Tonight she wore a clingy white sweater dress with an embroidered black velvet bolero jacket. Her mother hated this dress, which is what Sarah loved the most about it.

A short man wearing a tweed jacket, jeans, and a pair of John Lennon–style wire-rimmed glasses approached her.

"How are you?"

"Better than anyone you've ever had," she responded without missing a beat. Her smile was superior as she walked away to the bathroom.

Locking the door behind her, she removed a small brown bottle with a tiny silver spoon attached. She hated to share.

She found the mouse huddled near the entrance to the town house, apparently trying to either escape or disappear into the woodwork. Now that she looked at her closely, she decided Lisa really did look like a mouse—even her clothes were brown. She wore some sort of nondescript pants and an obviously expensive, totally unimpressive taupe sweater. And functional cold-weather boots. Sarah stifled a giggle.

"You've got to get yourself a new wardrobe, Lisa," Sarah said. "You're looking a little dowdy this evening."

Lisa knew Sarah was right, but she didn't comment, and in a few minutes, the other girl drifted off, apparently on her way to the bathroom again.

People were now crowding each other, fighting for turns at the coffee table. Someone was rolling up a bill into a tight cylinder and passing it to others to use. A girl who didn't seem older than sixteen licked her forefinger and dipped it into the white powder, then ran it along her gums. Lisa was tired and disgusted.

Just then Sarah drifted back. Her eyes were bright and dangerous as she made her way over to a man standing at the stairway. Lisa decided she'd grab Sarah quickly before she got entangled with the man.

"Do you mind if we go back. . . . I want to do some writing tonight."

Sarah dragged her smokey eyes away from the stranger whose name she could not recall. She had always wondered how Lisa's roommate, who seemed very cool in her articles, could possibly stand to live five years with this drip.

"Don't you tell me you want to leave already?" Sarah demanded. *"You* can leave if you want," she scoffed. "Go back to my dorm and bury yourself in your books and papers, Lisa, but you're never going to meet anyone that way."

Lisa felt a flash of indecision.

"It isn't even midnight yet," Sarah went on, taking a gulp of beer.

The party was cycling to its peak.

"I'm going to do a line," Sarah slurred under her breath. "I feel a little tipsy . . . then let's stop for five minutes at Dobie's—he's another friend who's always good for a few laughs. I'll meet you in the car."

———

Sarah fumbled as she put the key into the ignition.

"I think I should drive, Sarah."

"I'm fine, Lisa," Sarah said, squealing the BMW into the street and through the first stop sign. It was difficult to see. Salt from the winter streets spackled the car's windows.

"You'd better slow down," Lisa said.

"Relax. . . ." Sarah turned the corner and her wheels spun on the icy street. The breeze from the Hudson River turned Poughkeepsie's streets into ice sheets this time of year. Sarah's tires whirled and whined. Frustrated, she pressed the accelerator down to the floor.

"Sarah . . ."

"Shut up, Lisa."

Lisa bit her tongue. She ran her gloved hand over the window next to her just as a shadowy form came into view. Sarah's BMW careened crazily into the street.

"Shit . . . !" The car slid out of control.

"Watch out!" Lisa screamed.

Sarah jammed on the brake. The car spun.

There was a frightening thump.

The BMW flew over the curb on the opposite side of the narrow street and stalled. Both girls jerked backward from the momentum.

"Oh my God . . . you've hit someone!"

Sarah's head was just clear enough now for her to know that she wasn't thinking straight. She restarted the car and backed up to where they had heard the thump. Oddly enough, she didn't feel scared.

The defroster cleared the mist from the windows and now they saw the body lying motionless in the street. How long before the cops come? Sarah wondered. She looked up to the windows of the houses nearby to see if anyone had witnessed the accident. That's what she was already calling it in her mind—"The Accident"—something her father would have been able to fix and make go away.

Lisa clutched her arm, "Don't get out. What if he's dead?"

"I don't know," Sarah snapped, opening the door. Around the body there was a blitz of tiny fragments from her shattered headlights. Sarah thought the police could trace her car that way. She forced herself to look at the body that lay sprawled on the cold and icy pavement. Now it became real to her.

"Come on!" Lisa screamed.

"I think he's dead," Sarah said, her voice quivering.

He was just a boy, and his eyes were open and staring upward glassily. The frigid breeze blew over the Hudson and the cold was so intense it seemed to bite Sarah's flesh like the sharp teeth of an animal. She looked into the distance, and saw the lights of the Mid-Hudson Bridge. She thought about escape.

"Oh no," Lisa sobbed, nausea coming up the back of her throat. "Oh no, no . . . what are we going to do?"

"We've got to get out of here." Sarah threw herself back into the BMW, not daring to look back at the freezing motionless form. In the distance Sarah imagined she heard a siren wailing as she drove away.

It took a minute for the warmth of the car to penetrate Sarah's freezing bones. Next to her Lisa moaned, "We should call the police . . . you have to report an accident."

"Are you crazy? We have to get out of this. We could be in big-time trouble—our futures could be ruined." Sarah was driving fairly carefully now and she kept her eyes on the road.

Separately they were each beginning to realize the grim reality of the situation. They had been drinking. There were drugs in the car.

Lisa stared ahead, eyes filling.

Sarah stopped in front of her dorm and switched off the engine.

They sat in silence for several long minutes. Then: "What are we going to do?" Lisa asked.

"*You* are going into that dorm, into my room, and going to sleep. If anybody asks, you just say I'm spending the night with some guy I met at Patrick's. Nobody'll think twice about it."

"And what will you do?"

"I don't know. I'll let my mother figure something out."

"Sarah, the police should—"

"No police, Lisa. I don't know about you and the miserable life you lead in New York, but as for me, I like my freedom and I plan to keep it."

Slowly, the truth of what Sarah was saying was accepted by Lisa as well, and the wayward college girl could read it in her eyes. "I think we should make a solemn promise to each other," she said, "that we will never tell anyone about what happened tonight except my mother. She's the only person who needs to know. Now promise."

Lisa hesitated, then: "I promise."

———

Sarah took Highway 84 to her mother's home in Greenwich, avoiding the police traps on the Thruway. She had sobered up real quickly, but she didn't want to risk being put through a sobriety test. The state troopers made a sport of stopping vehicles just to check.

She glanced around the familiar sitting room. There were the bowls of fresh rosebuds, perfectly arranged on every table. There were her mother's needlepoint pillows, four sofas covered in chintz, the silver-framed photographs of her mother and her father. And there was Adele Potter, sitting reading a magazine, fully clothed and made up as if it were time to go to a ladies luncheon. When Sarah had awakened her earlier, she knew her mother would immediately get dressed, for company, which is what she considered her daughter.

"I've just returned from Palm Beach, you know, and it isn't what it used to be," Adele began. Sarah had told her mother nothing over the phone except that she was driving home, immediately. The obvious inference was that something was wrong since Sarah rarely came home at all, and never on a cold winter's weekend night. But here she was, Sarah marveled, talking as if everything were perfectly normal!

"It's a fortune for a room at the Breakers, a room, not a suite, mind you," she went on. "And you should see the kind of people they're letting stay there now. All those ghastly common nouveau riche types."

Sarah nodded, waiting for the moment when she could tell her own news, a moment that her mother was refusing to let occur.

"It's not at all what it once was, you know, when your father and I—"

"Oh Mother, so what! Who gives a damn!" Sarah burst in impatiently.

Adele looked at her daughter with surprise. She considered retorting sharply to Sarah's rudeness, but then decided to pretend she hadn't heard.

"People of our class . . ."

"Your class or mine?" Sarah interrupted. "I'm so tired of hearing this stuff!"

Adele's eyebrows arched and her entire body stiffened with the effort to keep her temper. "You came here in the middle of the night, Sarah. I presume you have a reason for it so please tell me what it is. I'm tired and I'd like to go back to bed."

"Forgive me, Mother dear, for interrupting the sleep you need for your active social life of club luncheons, but . . ." She breathed in deeply, looked away from her mother, then back at her.

"Sarah—?"

"I had a car accident."

"You seem all right. Why would that get you to come here in the middle of the night? I don't understand."

"I'm not hurt, Mother."

Adele started to rise from her chair, confused but relieved. "Well, then, I'll be off—"

"I killed someone. Accidentally, of course, but I hit someone and now he's dead and I drove away."

The magazine Adele had been holding slipped from her

grasp and fell to the floor as she sat back down again. She stared at her daughter, a frown creasing her face, her full lips pressed together. "I . . . I don't understand."

Sarah exploded. "What do you mean you don't understand? Can't you speak English? Are you deaf? I hit someone, killed him, drove away from the scene! Do you hear that! Do you understand it!"

"Sarah—"

"I need help, damn it! I need Daddy!" And finally, Sarah started to cry . . . whether for the loss of her father or for her actions that night, neither she nor her mother was quite sure. . . .

———

When her father died, security went out of Sarah's life. He had been struck down by cancer last year, and she still couldn't accept it. She had thought that a man as strong and vital and special as her father had to be immortal, like any god.

She remembered how cool and dim it had been in the funeral parlor, and the strange, sickly sweet odor that made her nauseous. The day of the church service, a fleet of Cadillacs, shiny, long, and black, sat idling out in front of the Episcopal church. There were so many strangers. Shoulders touching, breaths mingling into one giant sigh for their loss. The reverend offered to the Lord familiar words that the occasion called for, yet Sarah's father's death hadn't been for the best, she had thought then.

He had been the man who could entice her for hours with his storytelling. He had always taken care of her. She remembered collecting and arranging huge piles of red and gold maple leaves that had fallen from the trees. She had fashioned them into bedrooms and living rooms out on the lawn, and then she would walk through them with her father.

There would no longer be his strong hands to reach out and lift her; no more his energy. Her father was gone now, and her life was framed by his absence. Unconsciously, she let other men fill in for him. But not this time. This time there would be no easy fix for the trouble Sarah was in.

Adele Potter's patrician profile was stern beneath the subtle rose light that emanated from the antique Tiffany lamp that was one of many heirlooms Sarah knew would be hers one day. As though she cared. Sarah didn't care about things. She cared about fun and she cared about money. Her mother kept her eyes away from her daughter as she spoke:

"I'll call my brother. I have no choice," Adele said. "He will know how to best handle this."

"Oh, thank . . ."

"I'm not finished yet."

Now Adele turned and her sharp eyes crackled—the only sign of her anger. Her voice stayed low and modulated and Sarah knew it was because her mother had been trained to speak so servants couldn't hear. "I don't want to know what happens after this, Sarah. I suspect we can get you 'off the hook' as they say, but after that, you're on your own. I don't want to hear from you. I won't pay your way through school. You will be forced to make a life for yourself. I will not be here for you and I want you to disappear. I only hope you use the opportunity to make something decent out of yourself. God knows I've failed."

Now Sarah was really scared. Her father would never have done this, ever, no matter what kind of trouble she was in.

Sarah said nothing to her mother, thinking only that she had killed two people tonight: the stranger in the road, and herself. Without the Potter reputation and money, Sarah might as well be dead, too.

CHAPTER 7

Over the next few weeks, Kate started lunching regularly at Seasons, so she could be close to Christine. They had begun to talk endlessly on the telephone, recounting details of every lunch and dinner they attended. Whenever Christine told Kate she had to hang up and get back to work, Kate seemed not to hear. It would have been impossible for Christine to get rid of Kate, even if she had wanted to; however, she didn't want to. Christine was amused by Kate. They had fun conversations. Kate could swear like a drunken sailor, and drank like one, too. They laughed and laughed. Christine was delighted to have a friend. Kate was impregnable to friendship, but treasured their relationship for its professional and social benefits.

Kate had invited Christine to the Colony for lunch because Christine hadn't let her pay her tab at Seasons, ever since she had asked Kate to find out all she could about the mysterious man who had told her his name was Mark Althorp.

The two girls lay on lounge chairs near the pool, with their salads on a table in between them. The morning papers from New York, Los Angeles, and Washington were underneath a side table.

"I have some information for you," said Kate, undoing the strings on the bra of her bathing suit.

"As I told you before, Mark's real name is Ned Cooper. He is extremely wealthy and has made his money from various business ventures. He usually ruins his competitors for the sport of it. He also married a great deal of money, and rumor is, his marriage has not been a happy one. Her time is taken up with fashionable charities and cultural activities. They have no children."

"I was aware of all that," Christine said.

"Well, I don't think you are aware who his best friend and business partner is," Kate said.

"Who?"

"Alfred Blum."

Christine looked as if someone had slapped her. She was at a loss for words.

Kate studied Christine a long time before she spoke again. Whenever she asked questions about Alfred, Christine became silent and aloof.

"Do you think the two of them had some plan?" she asked finally.

"No, I do not believe that," Christine replied, shaking her

head emphatically. How ironic that it was a man she'd run into on the plane by happenstance who put her in touch with Blum. For all she knew, Alfred might have been aware of her through Mark—or Ned as she was learning to refer to him in her mind—all along.

"You have to admit it's a possibility," Kate said quietly.

Christine's face turned red, and her voice, when she spoke again, had a harsh tone.

"Alfred couldn't have been part of that," she said, measuring each word. She was unwilling to be drawn into a conversation about her business relationship with Blum.

Christine seemed close to tears. "I've got to get back to the hotel."

"You haven't finished your salad."

"I'm sorry. I've really got to get back." Christine rose to her feet.

"It might make you feel better to know that Ned Cooper supposedly never has affairs. You must have been special," Kate went on, trying to get her to stay.

"Thanks," Christine said dully.

"Listen, I'll try and find out more about their friendship. Ned is easier to research than Alfred," Kate said. "Is there anything about Blum's personal life that could be a start for me?"

"Not that I can think of. He's very tight-lipped."

"Are there any children?"

"No . . . his only son was killed in a hit-and-run accident in college."

"Where about?" said Kate, picking up her spiral notepad from the table.

"Somewhere in New York, I think."

"I'll call you after my interview with Garrison this afternoon," said Kate, squeezing Christine's hand. "Are you okay?"

Christine did not hear or feel. Her mind was elsewhere.

Kate was stunned. Garrison's secretary had just phoned and changed the location of their interview from Doherty's Restaurant to his home on North Ocean Boulevard. She could not believe she was going to the Morton mansion.

Kate smiled to herself. As always, she had thoroughly researched her prey. She had dozens of pictures of Garrison Morton in her hotel room, and she had cut out hundreds of clippings of articles on him and his family. He loved to travel to exotic locations; he was an avid tennis and golf player; he usually drinks only gin martinis; he values his privacy; and rumor around town was he was an excellent lover. She hoped the latter was true.

After prolonged fussing and spinning in front of the mirror, she was at last satisfied she looked great.

Kate announced herself through the intercom at the wrought-iron gates that were opened inside by the butler with what Kate assumed was a remote-control device. He also instructed her that Mr. Morton was awaiting her at the tennis courts. She parked next to Garrison's bright red Lamborghini in front of the two-story Spanish-style house and walked under enormous banyan trees that formed an arc of shade on the path. When she reached the court, she could see the expansive rear lawn that reached to the ocean and was covered with avocado, grapefruit, orange, and coconut palm trees. Pink and salmon bougainvillaea rioted everywhere along the fences. She watched the tall, confident figure dressed in tennis whites walk toward her. He seemed so at home in the beautiful setting, yet he had the look of a young boy still open to the enchantment of the unexpected.

Garrison Morton had been born into a great deal of wealth. He was in his mid-thirties, a bachelor, and a graduate of Harvard. He had not followed the family tradition of merchant banking; much to his mother's dismay, he had studied law, then chose not to practice it. He was a playboy and a wanderer, spending very little time in Palm Beach. He hated charity balls and stuffy dinners. He wanted only to enjoy life. He had a grasp of several languages and traveled the world, living a life of leisure, which he could well afford.

Garrison Morton was six feet two inches tall, slim, athletic, ruggedly handsome, with piercing green eyes. He was riveting.

"Let's go inside . . . it's too warm out here," he said in a strong voice.

Garrison led the way to the house and into the living room, where ceiling fans revolved slowly. There were two deep-tufted sofas piled high with tapestry pillows, and bookcases along one wall, full of volumes bound in red Moroccan leather with gold lettering.

"Congratulations, I read that you won the member guest tennis tournament at the Bath and Tennis," Kate said.

"Thank you. You play tennis?"

"I'm just beginning to play, although I've followed the game for years as a fan."

"May I get you a drink?" he asked.

"Whatever you're having will be fine."

From a portable bar he mixed two vodkas and orange juice, then motioned for her to sit down on the sofa.

"Tell me about your trip to China a few months ago. I've never been to that part of the world," she began, giving him her absolute attention.

Kate was determined to fascinate him with her wit and charm. She knew exactly how to praise and build up the male ego. She was bright and bewitching, and she knew it. All she had to do was get *him* to know it.

"There you are." A woman suddenly walked into the living room, her eyes peering sharply at Kate.

Kate immediately recognized Helen Morton, the matriarch of the clan. She was in her late seventies, with soft, snow-white hair that was impeccably coifed. Ice cold blue eyes confirmed what Kate had heard about her: She was, despite her age, as tough as nails, and as ungiving. Kate was both challenged and intimidated.

"Mother, this is Kate Robinson," Garrison said, immediately rising.

Mrs. Morton deliberately avoided Kate by pretending to adjust a painting that was hanging perfectly.

There was an awkward silence in the room.

"I expect *you* for dinner at eight, Garrison. It would mean a great deal to me," she added, then left as silently and abruptly as she had arrived.

"I guess she liked me," Kate remarked dryly after she was gone.

"Don't worry about it. Now you see why I travel so much," he laughed.

"It's your lot in life," she smiled.

He shook his head ruefully, then looked at Kate hard, studying her. She did not flinch under the scrutiny, knowing that he was thinking how totally inappropriate she was for him. How much his mother would hate her. How much he was attracted to her. Kate wanted to grin with the victory, but she managed to control herself.

"Would you care to join me for dinner tonight?" he suddenly asked.

She didn't hesitate a second. "I'd love to."

Garrison took her hand and raised it to his lips. The pressure of his mouth in her palm was more passionate a statement than anything he could say.

CHAPTER 8

$\mathcal{J}$essie lay stretched out on the bed, her eyes closed. Jake had gone over to a friend's house to watch a basketball game.

She knew he would want to make love when he got home, and she had begun to dread even that. Their bedroom could not contain the hostilities of its tenants—Jake's angry outbursts and sniping criticisms, and Jessie's stoicism followed by uncontrollable weeping. She used to enjoy making love with Jake, but lately she preferred to be alone with her fantasies. She really didn't know how good or bad their sex life was since she had no way of making comparisons. Jessie had been a virgin when she met Jake—Raymond was careful not to go that far—and he was the only man she had ever been with. She had no idea what she needed; Jake never asked her what she needed. He only criticized her for fantasizing. Jake had filled her with self-doubt concerning her sexuality when she told him she had visualized herself in other situations. Now she always held herself back. She couldn't help it. She could go through the motions, but when it was over, resentment would hit her.

Jessie needed to make believe. She could not deny to herself that the prospect of experiencing sex with another man titillated her.

She loved the idea of a man stealing into her room and making exquisite love to her. Dashing, forceful, but tender.

Jessie began to touch herself gently as she mentally sketched out her scenario.

It was very late when Jake entered the bedroom, but she was still awake. There were strips of street light forming glowing bands across the bed.

"The game went into overtime," he said, as he undid his buckle and his pants with rapid precision.

She lay back on the pillow, watching him, holding the blanket clutched at her throat to cover her body.

"Are you okay?" he asked, turning on the lamp.

"What? Oh, yes, yes," she said absently as Jake sat down on the edge of the bed to remove his shoes.

"I thought we could have a talk," she finally began quietly.

"I do not want my wife working," he stated irritably, "if that's going to be our topic." Jake did not look at her.

"Please don't be like this, Jake. There are *two* people in this marriage, in case you haven't noticed." She was throwing her pleas at a mind that could not be reached.

"I told you I want you at home where you belong."

Jessie tried to think of something to say. Something to convince him there was nothing wrong with her working part-time. She felt as if she were leading her whole life one step at a time, trying not to think of the length of a hopeless road.

"Well, then, maybe I could try to sell some of my paintings in one of the galleries."

"Don't be silly, Jessie . . . you'd make a fool of yourself."

And then Jake was taking off her pajamas while she lay staring up at the ceiling. There were no endearments in their love-making, not even any kissing.

He touched her breasts. She felt nothing. His hand moved from her breasts to between her legs, as if stressing his ownership. She was already wet; she had had an orgasm by her own hands. She wondered in a detached way if he attributed her readiness to his inadequate foreplay. She put her mind somewhere else, with someone else whose face she did not yet know. He entered her abruptly, and with force. She heard him moan, felt his breath, then the shudder of his orgasm.

Jake dropped back on his pillow and lay still.

"What were you thinking about, Jessie?"

"You," she lied.

———

Jessie stood at the door of the art gallery, with the sun trickling down through the palm fronds, and she watched the motion of the light over a stillness where nothing else moved. It was an odd, solemn stillness, giving her the sudden certainty that she was facing the approach of something unknown and of the gravest importance. She had awakened this morning with a feeling of confidence, a sense she could finally venture forth.

She had dropped Allison off at Wee Wisdom Day Care and driven directly to Worth Avenue. She had come to this gallery three times before, but she never had had the courage to go in. She had decided to work part-time, and to try and show her paintings—without Jake's permission. She had never outright defied him about anything before, but she was doing so now. Her identity had become something Jake had carved out for her, and she was sick and tired of it.

Jessie walked back to the car and opened the trunk, where she had carefully placed three of her paintings between blankets. She smiled. Her work gave her the calm she needed. She had started when Allison was a baby without conscious intention, but she saw her art grow under her hands, pulling her forward, giving her a healing sense of peace. Maria had been helpful—the psychic had boosted her fragile belief in her own talents. Now she understood that what she needed was the motion of some purpose, besides wife and mother —no matter how small or in what form. Jake liked to think of himself as her guardian, her conscience. "You will be depriving our child of her mother," his words rang in her ear. Stop it—she told herself with quiet severity.

"Do you want to bring these inside?" asked the secretary. "No one will be here until ten." The secretary was a fat, pallid woman who moved with effort.

"Yes . . . thank you," Jessie replied, lifting up one of her seascapes and carrying it inside.

In the doorway of the Barkly Art Gallery, Jessie felt a faint touch of anxiety looking around at all the other artwork. She forced herself to bring in the other two paintings, and propped them up against one wall. She thought often of Maria. Was there really a subtle message of an inspired nature from some unknown source that leads to new paths? That was what the psychic had recently told her, and she had felt it more clearly than ever this morning: a smiling sense of hope within her, the certainty her work held promise.

She was barely aware of the person that came through the door as she was looking at the picture she had titled "Life and Death." It was a globe half in light, half in shade. Poised above it was a calm and noble face—a face on which youth, health, hope, love all shone with ineffable radiance.

"How beautiful. Do you imagine that the face of a woman?"

"Actual beauty is sexless," Jessie replied slowly, turning.

"Forgive me . . . I startled you," he said, extending his hand. "My name is Ned Cooper."

The man before her was tall and his broad shoulders emphasized how slender he was. His face was cut by prominent cheekbones and he had bold, piercing, arrogant eyes that were alert and intelligent. His expression was proud and challenging, his posture erect and assured. He held his head in the manner of one who takes his beauty for granted, but knows others do not. He was riveting and irresistible to look at. She was in a daze.

"Is this your work?" he asked.

"Yes," she whispered.

"I like it."

"Really?"

He looked at her for a moment, his eyes narrowing. He

did not name the nature of his own feeling to himself—he never did. He tried to never identify emotions. This was a steadfast rule of his. He only wanted to feel. That was the only identification he cared to know.

"Listen, a friend of mine is having an exhibit of new artists from the area tomorrow night. I'll call him and tell him to expect you. Tomorrow, seven P.M., at Seasons."

She was about to utter a protest, when he stopped her by gently touching her shoulder.

"I'll see you tomorrow," he said, then his tall figure moved out the door with the unstressed, unhurried confidence of habitual authority.

Ned Cooper decided to forget about the painting he was going to purchase and instead walked back up to the ocean block of Worth Avenue to his office. He entered the white stucco building and proceeded directly to his penthouse suite. At the window, he looked down at the miles of unspoiled, snowy-white beach. A white sun beat down on the electric blue water. Ned had seen many beautiful women in his life, but the clean, proud strength in the face of the woman he had just met at the gallery fully occupied his mind.

Ned Cooper III had been born to inherit an empire. His great-grandfather had planned it that way. Ned Sr. had been a self-made man, who by dint of a sharp brain had developed the Cooper sleeping pill. The rest was history. Cooper & Cooper was now a huge corporate empire.

Ned's early childhood had been a happy one, running free in the Palm Beach mansion, with its big, sunny, walled gardens. All his childhood friends lived exactly the same way.

His mother loved him and his father was determined to have him follow him in the family business, as he had followed his own father. He worked himself up the ladder, learning everything. He made few real friends in life, simply because his work satisfied most every need for him. Nothing and no one would make him deviate from his responsibility. His father had expected him to prove his worth; as his heir, he would be undertaking great responsibility, and he had done just that upon his death. Ned was now president of Cooper & Cooper, and he was only thirty-seven years old.

He was at work every day before seven, going over each and every detail of the business, drafting plans for new ways to expand in some areas, conserve in others, deciding where to cut back and how to maximize profits. He drew up plans to send his executives to other countries to facilitate new plants. He used his business school knowledge to re-structure the whole financial base of the Cooper empire, planning new investments into industry and real estate. He earned a reputation as a man to be reckoned with. Ned's iron hand and steely brain controlled his business world expertly.

Ned Cooper was a very complicated man, at once ruthless and compassionate. He could take away someone's family business without batting an eyelash, yet he gave millions of dollars to various charities, and financed the education of scores of his employees' children, demanding total anonym-ity. He could be very rude, but then he could draw people to him with his innate charm. He could be a fabulous friend; he could be just as bad an enemy. He was viewed by many as a mysterious and frightening figure. His urge to control made him a notoriously difficult boss or partner. Nothing—not family, friends, or love could come between him and his work.

He remembered nothing distinct of the past twenty years. They were blurred, like a streak of space. His life was ordered with no room to hesitate. He had moved toward his goals, sweeping aside everything that did not pertain to them. He had not allowed many women in his life, and when he wanted sex, he found it efficient to pay for it, always using the name Mark Althorp.

It was the utter perfection of the union that drove him to marriage to Cornelia. What mattered was that two business empires—two huge fortunes merging—would increase the prominence and influence of both families.

When Ned's father had suggested a premarital agreement be signed, Cornelia's father had tossed it in his face. The affront of being asked had been an insult, he insisted. So the marriage took place without one. They were immediately known as *the* couple in the world of wealth and power.

It wasn't until a month into the marriage that Ned learned why Cornelia's father had made sure it would be very difficult to divorce his daughter. Cornelia was a lesbian.

After a lifetime in Palm Beach, observing the mixing and matching of egos and libidos that swirled around town, Ned thought he was unfazed by any sexual combination. He had a varied sexual appetite himself. However, the sight of his wife and her social secretary in bed together, making love, was too grotesque to abide. And because Cornelia knew divorce was financially impossible, she and her lover reveled in exhibitionism at home. They sunbathed nude; they strolled naked through the gardens.

Ned could not believe she favored a woman over him, so he put himself even more into his work. They both performed well in their public roles of devoted husband and wife. When they entertained, there was never a hint of a masquerade being enacted. Privately, each went his own way. And currently, the lovely woman from the gallery was the way he wished to go.

There had been very few times when women had mattered. He liked anonymous sex; he liked masks. He had learned from Christine that it was important never to look into the face of his lover, or he might lose control. Her power over him was concentrated in those dark eyes, and once caught in them, he had weakened. The last night in London, he had given in to his great passion for her. In that moment, she held the cards and he had nearly paid the price for it— real feeling was dangerous. He'd best remember that now.

CHAPTER 9

*J*essie finished washing the dishes and sat down at the kitchen table. Allison was getting her pajamas on. Once again, Jake had not come home for dinner nor had he called. He was drinking too often and too much, but Jessie never said anything about it. When they were alone together they sat silently—the silence louder than any words. She had been so excited about sharing the news of her first exhibition, but she was kidding herself to think that Jake was the one with whom to share it. It would have to wait. She looked at her watch. It was nine-fifteen; she couldn't keep Allison up any longer. She would tuck her in alone—again.

Jessie stopped momentarily at the bedroom door; she could hear Allison talking to her imaginary playmate. Her voice was soft music, her words like gentle tinkling. The minute Jessie entered the room, Allison ran leaping into her bed. The two lay down together—it was their ritual. Allison lay her head in the well of her mother's arm. Every night, Allison wanted to be told the story of the pregnancy and her birth. She always asked the same questions. She had an insatiable craving to know about every detail.

". . . then the doctor could see your hair . . ."

The white sheet was pulled up to their necks.

"What next, Mommy? Did you know I was a girl?" she asked, scooting in a little closer.

Afterward, Jessie lay with her daughter asleep beside her, thinking. The orange tree outside the window cast a delicate fragrance on the warm, delicious night air. The moon lit up the room in a soft haze. Jessie sighed. Where was he?

It was two A.M. when she heard the front door. Jessie tiptoed out of the room.

"Where have you been, Jake?"

A silence followed, a long and weighted one.

"Out," he replied finally, looking steadfastly at Jessie with bloodshot eyes, and alcoholic insolence. "Warm me up some dinner," he ordered, opening the refrigerator door.

She shook her head in disbelief. "This is not a diner, Jake. Dinner was ready at six, like always."

"I don't give a shit about that. You have nothin' to do all day while Allison is in school, so you can damn well make me some dinner now!"

Jessie squeezed her fingernails into her palms. She held them that way long enough for her world to quiet down.

"I was *very* busy today, Jake. I took some of my paintings

to Worth Avenue. As a matter of fact, I have my first exhibition tomorrow night." She started to pace. "I planned a celebration for the three of us at dinner. . . . The champagne is still in the ice bucket."

Jake was breathing like a steam engine.

"I thought this painting bullshit was all settled. I forbid you to work!"

Their two shadows clashed and crossed on the ceiling like swords.

"Don't tell me what to do, Jake. Do you hear me?" she said with force. "Don't ever tell me what to do again!"

"I'll tell you exactly what to do, you're *my* wife!" he yelled, catching her arm in a resolute grip. The muscles of his neck bulged like ropes.

With a violent effort, Jessie wrenched her arm from his clasp. She seethed with pent-up anxiety and anger.

"I will decide what I'm going to do, Jake. You don't know what I need or want. And I've decided to work!" she let her words explode in the air.

"Goddamnit, Jessie, I said no!"

"Stop it, Jake!" she screamed. Her eyes opened wide as she saw Allison appear in the doorway.

"What's wrong?" cried Allison, her blue eyes shining like a crystalline pond, tears streaming down her face.

"It's all right, honey, it's nothing," Jessie started to say, her voice softening, but Jake cut her off.

"Yes, it's something if you will not be here to take care of your daughter! Tell your daughter your painting is more important than she is."

"Stop it, Jake." Her eyes flashed a warning to him, as she went toward Allison. The longing she saw in those eyes was bottomless. A plea barely in control. She hugged her little girl, her breath finally steadying. She looked at Jake. She had no idea how they reached this terrible place in their relationship. This was not the man she had married.

"I'm sleeping with Allison tonight," she stated, and before Jake could say another word, she lifted her daughter in her arms and stormed into Allison's room, slamming and locking the door in Jake's enraged face.

―――――――

Jessie's hand trembled a little and she spilled a few drops of her perfume on the floor. She was exhausted, having been up half the night trying to calm Allison who was now outside playing. Jake was late again, as usual. They hadn't spoken to each other all day.

It was six-forty-five. She couldn't wait much longer.

She heard the back door.

"Where have you been? I'm going to be late!"

"I stopped to see if Nancy could babysit. . . . I thought I'd step over to your show for a little bit."

"Really?"

"Yeah."

"You promise?"

"Yeah."

Jessie took a step toward him.

"That would mean a great deal to me, Jake."

"Well, you go ahead. I'll be there as soon as I shower."

"Okay, see you soon. And thank you."

―――――――

In the lobby of Seasons, Christine had removed her original oil paintings, and elegantly illuminated the new artists' works by muted light. The room was festooned with orchids and tiger lilies.

"Hello, I'm Christine Wells." She extended her hand to Jessie in greeting.

"Hello. I'm Jessie Malcolm. I'm—"

"You're one of the new artists," Christine said. "Of course, welcome. I'm very pleased to show your work at my hotel. In fact, one of your paintings was sold this afternoon to an anonymous caller. . . . Congratulations!"

"Oh my goodness, how exciting!" Jessie was beside herself.

"I'm sorry I've got to go to a business dinner; however, I'm sure we'll see each other again. And I'll be sending you a check for a thousand dollars," Christine told her.

"A thousand dollars?" Jessie couldn't believe it. After Christine left, a smile stayed on Jessie's face as she moved through the crowd. She didn't know a soul, but it didn't matter. Her paintings were being seen for the first time, *and* her first one had been sold. What more could she want! She wondered a moment who the buyer could be. If she had asked Christine, she would have answered Mark Althorp.

Over the next hour, she forced herself to make small talk with the strangers while she watched the entrance for Jake. Where was he?

Deciding to take a break, she wandered through the dining room and out to the garden. Another broken promise, she thought. But she wouldn't let it spoil her happiness this evening.

Then she walked back into the party, and the only thing left of the tears she had tried to hold back in the darkness of the garden was a fiercely luminous sparkle in her eyes.

Ned's eyes swept over the crowd swiftly, in the manner of a prowler with a flashlight. He had arrived, purposely, just as the showing was ending. He loathed parties, and he attended, reluctantly, a few social occasions in Palm Beach, and only when he was invited by men with whom he did business. He had long tried to keep himself off the front pages, for his power rested in back-channel maneuvering. However, tonight he was here for Jessie. He wanted to see her; the desire had been intense and immediate.

All the women he knew seemed to resemble one another, with the same look of static grooming: thin eyebrows plucked to a certain lift, eyes frozen in mock amusement. All of them overdressing. He could sniff out pretension, false-ness, vanity, and fraud with the instinct of a killer. Then there was Jessie. She stood out. She was different.

She appeared wearing an absolutely plain dress. Her manner was as invitingly simple as her clothes. She looked at ease with what she was, who she was, and where she came from. He watched her move. She had an electric, effortless sensuality that was independent of age or gender. Mystery is the essential component of glamour, he often thought, and Jessie had that. Her only ornamentation was one silver bracelet. It gave her the most of all feminine aspects . . . the look of being chained.

Jessie stood by herself, aloof, clasping her bag in her hands, pretending to be regarding someone else's painting. She glanced to her right and saw him by the door. She looked away, yet a few minutes later, she found herself wait-ing for him to approach her. The moment had no ties to her past or future, only the immediate intensity of the feeling that she was imprisoned alone with him, in this room. She found it difficult to breathe.

———

Ned watched a stranger approach her. He felt a twisting pain; it was jealousy of every man who spoke to her, or looked at her. He had never felt anything like this before. A smile stayed on her face as she moved through the crowd, a fluid smile that ran into the look of boredom worn by all the faces around her.

"Hello, Jessie," Ned said, finally approaching her.

"Hello. And thank you for making all this possible."

"Are you ready to leave?" he said simply.

Their eyes locked and then, without further hesitation, she nodded.

When they reached the highway, Ned speeded up, and Jessie watched his hands on the steering wheel. He drove with a smooth, dangerous confidence. She liked the power of the Ferrari convertible sailing down the highway. She claimed that power for the moment, attaching herself to it somehow. For just a while, for as long as it lasted, she wanted to surrender completely—to forget everything and just *feel*. She shook her head dazedly. She wanted to forget Jake . . . and the marriage. The stress of her situation with him was unendurable.

Ned parked the car on a deserted stretch of road near the beach. They removed their shoes, and he got a blanket from the trunk.

"Come with me," he said quietly, leading her to the beach.

The hand guiding her was strong. And the yellow moon was an arc illuminating the two of them.

Try as he might to resist looking at her, his glance moved

of its own accord slowly up the line of her long legs, to her dress—to her eyes. He felt he could see straight through her clothes, and through her mind. They were not holding hands, but their shadows in the sand were. The water lapped gently at their feet.

She wanted him to touch her.

He moved in closer, wrapping her in his arms. She felt she would drown in a sea of want. She desired him without doubts or hesitation. Her mouth was half-open in helpless, begging expectation.

Then his lips were on hers, his fingers twisting into her long hair.

Soon she was naked. She stood utterly exposed in the moonlight, trembling as Ned appraised the long limbs, the gentle curves of her breasts, the flat smooth stomach.

He should have sensed the danger. He wanted her more than he had ever wanted any woman—even Christine.

He slipped his shirt off as his mouth kissed hers again with exquisite tenderness. He could feel her erect nipples against his bare chest, as his tongue filled her mouth. His eyes held hers.

His lips moved slowly down the curve of her throat below her ear, and his hands began to caress her breasts. His fingers lingered on her nipples, gently tracing circling patterns around them.

With sudden passionate hunger, he kissed her roughly on the mouth as his palm moved up the inside of her thigh. He gently cupped her most intimate place, moving his forefinger up and down in tiny sensual butterfly movements. Her body undulated against his.

He felt her heart pounding. She clung to him, panting, wet. Then he stepped away. She watched him undress. She watched his every movement. They gazed at each other, transfixed by the intensity of their desires. She slipped to the sand and he knelt over her.

"What do you want?" he whispered.

"I want you." And she started to close her eyes.

"Look at me," he said softly, gently inserting his finger inside her.

She began to move back and forth, her hand reaching down to touch his hardness.

For several minutes they played with each other. Then: "I want you inside me." Jessie's hoarse whisper was in his ear. "Now . . . please," she said, urging him on top of her and guiding him into her.

Barely sliding in and out, he teased her with a few exquisite strokes, entering . . . withdrawing . . . entering . . . withdrawing. . . .

Then he made exquisite love to her.

"Please," she cried. "Please."

At last, he thrust deeply into her, riding her, kissing her passionately. With long slow strokes he took her with a power and a hunger that left them both breathless. She moved faster, arching her back in overwhelming pleasure. He could hold back no longer, and he exploded into her with a long intense shudder, in the same instant her orgasm was spreading through her body.

Afterward, they lay silent, looking up at the stars, feeling no desire to move or think or know that there was anything beyond this moment.

Jessie lingered a moment to collect her courage to go in. Finally, she turned the key in the front door.

Jake sat slumped in a chair in the living room, his legs spread apart, his arms resting in two strict parallels on the arms of the chair. A patch of beer soaked the crotch of his shorts, as if his own discomfort were a revenge upon his wife. There was a long silence.

She locked him into her gaze until he looked down at the floor.

"Aren't you going to say anything, Jessie?"

She heard the question, but it had to wait its turn to enter the crowded path to her consciousness.

Could she do this to Allison?

Was it fair to her?

Was there even one shred of hope for this marriage?

That thought ended in an invisible shudder.

"Aren't you going to justify yourself, Jessie? It's one A.M. Where have you been?"

"I won't answer that, Jake."

"I want to know."

"I said I'm not going to answer that. It doesn't matter anymore." She hesitated. "I want you to move out, Jake. Allison is the one I need. You can go. She is the only one I have to have."

She shrugged her purse off her shoulder, put it on the sofa, and started toward Allison's bedroom.

"Just like that?" he asked in disbelief.

She merely looked at him. There was nothing left to say. When she had been angry, there was still hope. With indifference, there was nothing.

CHAPTER 10

Christine stood behind the reception desk going over some invoices, unaware of the group of people who had just arrived at cocktail hour.

"Are you Christine Wells?" a man came up and asked her. Without waiting for an answer, he went on. "My name is Lawton Dodd, and I'm with the Florida National Bank." He held out his hand and Christine took it, recognizing his name since the bank handled the hotel's accounts.

"It's nice to meet you," Christine said, coming out from behind the front desk. She had never personally met him, leaving that to Alfred. She wondered what was behind this sudden appearance.

"Would you care to join me for a drink?" he asked. "I apologize for not giving you advance notice, but I never seem to have time to call my own."

Christine smiled pleasantly. "I have some things to finish, but then I'd be happy to join you."

"Fine. I'll be in the bar."

Christine did not know that the banker was intending to use her. Even though his bank held Seasons's business account, all of Alfred Blum's personal accounts were deposited elsewhere. It would be a great coup to land Alfred Blum.

Lawton Dodd was twenty-eight years old and generally regarded as a successful young man; however, he wanted to do great things, magnificent things, things unsurpassed in . . . anything. He was charged with energy, too much energy, and always looking for a place to expend it. He was determined to carve a place in the world and make it his. He wanted power. He did not feel bound to his banking business, but he was good at it. Lawton knew he wasn't the brightest person in the world; his greatest talent was the way he could make friends instantly. He could smile with understanding at people over nothing at all. He could use a trip to the water cooler to pick out a potential customer with the soft, cheery glow of his eyes, making them feel they were the most important human being and his newest, dearest friend. He slipped into Palm Beach society with an eel-like ease, five years ago, after graduating from Tulane, deciding that Palm Beach money was a banker's fantasy.

Everybody in town loved Lawton. He always granted people a grandeur they had not earned. That was his biggest asset. Lawton would listen with breathless attention to women, not a word of which he ever remembered afterward. And he would listen with clever attention and open admiration to the men. He was incredibly canny and there was something of the Southern politician about him. He was unpretentious yet immediately compelling. He always punctuated a sentence with one's name, and the stamina with which he could sustain interest in other people's conversation, however dull, was unsurpassed. He knew all of his contacts were going to ease him up the ladder of success.

In the beginning, he mainly had the old dowagers' accounts; then, after learning all he could about several businessmen in town, he landed Ned Cooper. After that, he felt light as air, and saw the road to his future, clear and open. For him, no expenses were spared in entertaining the cream of Palm Beach society. Lawton was out every night.

A lean, attractive man with premature gray in his thick black hair, and intense polished steel eyes, Lawton's name had been linked with a number of glamorous women, yet he had no one special in his life. Usually, he never progressed beyond a few kisses. He knew he could have any woman; he just rarely took advantage of it. A lot of things were obscured by his considerable charm—even his bisexual tendencies. He understood the power of his charm. He knew it allowed him a graceful distance. And from that distance, he could maneuver well.

Christine was watching Lawton from across the room, curious about a man she heard about but never met.

Over the past months, she had been watching, learning, and listening. She attended the Chamber of Commerce meetings in both West Palm and Palm Beach. Lawton was president of the Palm Beach Chamber of Commerce, and was vocal against the entertainment industry doing any shooting

here. She voraciously read all of the local newspapers following every movement of the "A" crowd. She watched the
longing of the perpetual outsiders for the ultimate insiders.
She was mesmerized by the world of Palm Beach.

Suddenly, at this solitary moment, the past turned on her
like a revolving door. She shivered. She would bury it forever. She wanted to be one of the queens of Palm Beach
society. The white-hot desire for respectability burned
within her. She loved the taste, the smell, the feel of it.
Maybe Lawton Dodd could help her achieve it.

She walked into the bar. Lawton got to his feet and held
out the gray velveteen bucket chair for her at the black
lacquer-topped round cocktail table.

"Thanks for taking the time to meet with me," he began.

"I needed the break," she smiled, accepting her usual Per-
rier and lime from the young cocktail waitress.

"I'm sure you know your figures are very good for such a
new business," Lawton began. "And I was curious to meet
you. Alfred speaks so highly of you." If she continued as she
was doing, she would be profitable in six months. Her business acumen intrigued him. For a small establishment, her
hotel was doing extremely well—and she was devastatingly
attractive. She would be an asset on anyone's arm. If he
cultivated her intensively, clearly their friendship would
bring him closer to Alfred.

"Thank you. I am pleased with the way things are going,"
she said. "And I'm delighted to meet you, too. It's nice to
meet one's banker in person," she smiled.

"What do you think of Palm Beach?" he asked.

"I had enough of high society back in London. It can be
rather boring."

"Oh? What do your parents do?"

She winced. It was like a sudden blow from a great distance. Right behind the blow, something privately shameful seeped in.

"They were killed in a plane crash."

"I'm sorry, please excuse me, I didn't know."

"It's all right. . . . I just don't like to talk about it."

"By the way, Miss Wells . . ."

"Christine, please."

"Thank you. I've been invited to a small dinner party tomorrow night at Mrs. Frick's—she's the chairwoman of the Red Cross. Would you care to accompany me, Christine?"

Christine's pulse quickened, but she was careful not to act too interested.

"I'd love to," she said finally, calmly.

"Fine. I'll pick you up at eight then."

"I'll see you tomorrow."

Later, alone in her bedroom, she looked out the bay window. The moon went behind a cloud, and only a pale beam of radiance shone forth. Except for her work and her new friend Kate, Christine had been very much alone in these long, humid days. She was ecstatic at the mere thought of being invited into a level of society she had only dreamed of before. She couldn't wait to tell Kate. In her own way, Christine claimed Kate more ferociously than Kate ever claimed her. Their one-hour daily phone calls to each other were a ritual that bordered on the obsessive. Kate entertained her— she could be so theatrical. She could lend drama to the most mundane items. Christine loved that about her—the way she exaggerated things, injecting so much life and laughter.

She clung to her friend's magnetic orbit, telling her secrets of her own painful childhood. She found herself wanting to, liking it. Perhaps it was Kate's distance from the events, or her thirst for hearing about them. But tonight, she realized how lonely she had been, the kind of loneliness a best friend could not fill. She wanted a man. She hoped that man would be Lawton.

Lately, it had only been Alfred.

The call always came the same way: Alfred's manservant would ring and make the date. Then flowers would be delivered. Then Alfred would arrive in his limousine. Always, they met at Seasons in her suite, and always in the daytime. Their business was transacted at his office, their private dealings at the hotel.

Today, earlier, he had wanted her quickly. Alfred had an extraordinary sexual energy that seemed to feed on itself; he was more passionate the second time than the first, and so on. His love-making was ardent, expressing feelings Christine knew he compartmentalized from the rest of the world. She was aware that his wife was drinking herself to death and that this was hurting him. His love-making told her this. As ugly as he was, Alfred had a certain depth of character that she respected a great deal. In another life, she might have loved him, if there wasn't such a power struggle between them, if there wasn't her past as a weapon for him. At this point in their complex partnership, though, they were as equal as she could ever hope them to be. And so she chose this time to free herself.

The crushed velvet bedspread had been too warm and she resented the rough feel of it, but she didn't want to be undressed and vulnerable when she demanded her liberation. He had emerged from the suite's bathroom in the black terry robe she kept for him. They had made love once already, but he had reclaimed himself, and his face gave nothing away.

"Alfred, I want to end this . . . part of it," she began.

His voice was low and gave off no warning signs. "Trust me, Christine. You do not want to end this part of it yet. I may be even more useful to you in the future."

They both knew how much money Seasons was throwing off. Between them, there were pretenses and smoke screens, but not about business.

"What makes you say that?"

"Lawton. He was quite impressed—couldn't stop raving about you." He seemed to be changing the subject but she couldn't be sure.

"What does that have to do with what I'm saying?"

"Nothing, my dear Christine. Just that *I* will tell *you* when it's over."

She respected his gamesmanship enough to know there was a good reason he was denying her. Much, much later, she would realize the timing of the day's liaison was not a coincidence. By then it would be late in the game.

———

Over the next few weeks, Christine began to see Lawton on a regular basis. Life was beginning to take on a new glow, dimming the pain over Mark. Her soul's ambitions were becoming ferocious, and she was learning a lot from Lawton—just by watching him cater to the white-haired dowagers at social functions. There was a small flicker of hope that there was a life for them together. They had only one problem—their sex life. There was none. Christine could not believe it. With her gift for flattery, she could make a man feel as if he were Apollo. Lawton appeared sexually ambivalent.

She took the initiative one night and invited him upstairs to her room. She helped him undress. Then, as they lay naked under the cool satin sheets, she relaxed him through a prolonged and carefully modulated massage, with a brushing movement of the fingers, all over the nipples, stomach, and thighs, and after a deliberately protracted delay, finally the genitals.

She sighed, relieved. Through erotic games and massage, she finally satisfied him and earned a gratitude that would make him dependent on her. She was on her way . . . again.

CHAPTER 11

Kate sat waiting for Adele Parsons in the bar at the Colony. She had failed to show up for their last interview, and she hoped she wouldn't have to abandon this story. Her boss had hinted that her sources in Palm Beach may have dried up, wise to her now. Kate knew she needed a big break. Garrison Morton was probably her only chance, her only entrée to the old guard.

Over the past weeks, Kate had begun to receive invitation after invitation from Garrison. She had grasped shrewdly from the first moment she had looked into his eyes that he wanted a strong woman, and one that was not too available.

Her calculations were beginning to pay off. Garrison was unable to forget her. She pretended she was interested when he walked her through museums and galleries. She knew everything about the hobbies he liked. She listened as he spoke passionately about Shakespeare and Balzac. She knew how to make him laugh, and she would regale him with witty, risqué stories. However, when he asked her to go on a trip down the Nile, she turned him down, saying she had to meet with publishers who were interested in a novel she was writing. And when he had tried to make love to her, she also turned him down. The more interested he got, the more ambivalent she acted toward him. That had been difficult, since his reputation as a lover was second to none—and she was growing tired of being alone.

An hour and a half later, Kate went up to her room and told the secretary who answered the telephone at Mrs. Parsons's home "to go jump in the lake." What she couldn't believe was that Mrs. Parsons, a nouveau riche, passed up the second opportunity to be interviewed. She loved publicity; it made no sense.

Kate felt the panic. She knew her boss wanted her back in New York, but that was a dead end for her. She had to find a way to afford to stay in Palm Beach, and fulfill her real ambition: to write books. Maybe she would have to make an advantageous marriage. However, she would never turn into a rich obscurity; she wanted success. She opened her purse and took out yet another letter of rejection from another publisher. The repudiation of her artistry was more painful than she could imagine.

Unknown to anyone, even Christine, Kate had been writing a novel. At first she had tried sending off a hundred pages and an outline of a "sex and stripping" novel, not wanting to give up a percentage to an agent. She had made the mistake of assuming a book contract would be easy to land, based on her growing reputation as a journalist. But it hadn't happened that way; six publishers rejected it, one actually sending a form letter signed by an "assistant." Kate was still smarting over that. Didn't these people know who she was?

In the few months Kate had been gone, Lisa had turned the second bedroom into an office. "We both know you're not going to need this old place," Lisa said when Kate visited a few days later.

Kate remembered now why she had stayed so long with Lisa as her roommate. She was actually fond of the timid young woman and missed the sense of security that having someone inferior around always gave her. Palm Beach was paradise, but it was risky living there. You could fall so far from paradise.

Lisa had volunteered to get Kate together with her agent, a baby-faced man named Eric Rothstein who worked for Literary Enterprises, a medium-size agency that had merged with a large British talent management group and was now one of the hottest groups in New York City. Actually, Kate had met Rothstein a number of times over the five years she spent with Lisa and had been amazed that such an unimpressive-looking guy with a thick Brooklyn accent had managed to make a name for himself as a literary agent.

"What should I wear?" Kate asked, and Lisa visibly glowed under the attention. "You're better at this scene than I am. How about this?" The gray dress she held up was so sedate just looking at it on the hanger dampened Kate's ebullient mood.

"No, no way. What else did you bring? Your navy Chanel copy is still here, right?"

"Perfect idea." Kate threw Lisa a little kiss as she went to shower. "How am I going to make it in Palm Beach without you?"

Lisa laughed, but the compliment meant something to her.

In the bathroom, Kate stuck her tongue out at herself. "What a phoney you are." Her reflection smiled back at her from the mirror.

Rothstein was twelve minutes late. The midtown restaurant had very few tables set aside for cocktails only and the room was filling up with the drinks crowd. The pudgy-faced agent breezed in carrying the winter chill of February on his overcoat. Wool, Kate noticed, probably Paul Stuart. Very New York literary. Not yet earning enough for cashmere, she automatically calculated.

"Sorry I'm late. Have you ordered a drink for yourself?" Rothstein barely looked at her. His eyes scanned the room stopping to acknowledge silently a tall, brown-haired woman in her forties. The two waved and smiled. "Mona Ackerman—do you know her?" Rothstein said breezily, clearly indicating he was certain Kate knew no one.

"Actually, I submitted my novel to her. She was the one who suggested I seek representation. I think she might have mentioned your name." Silently, Kate prayed he would not see this for the out-and-out lie it was.

"Didn't you tell me Lisa Greene recommended me?"

God, did these people keep notes on their conversations or what? She could have kicked herself. She felt like a fool. As a journalist she should have known how much a mind can retain about small details when they are relevant to one's business. Her regard for the man shot up a notch. He only looked like he was not paying attention.

There was a large gap in the conversation that Kate did

not try to fill. Thankfully the waiter came over and they each ordered mineral water.

"Do you think that's what's changing the country?" Small talk—how she hated small talk.

"What's that?" The pudgy man absentmindedly removed a sesame pretzel stick from the bowl on the table.

"Water, no cocktails, light-fare lunches."

He smiled in his detached way, ate the pretzel, looked at his watch. "So, you're a gossip columnist."

Kate smiled but she hated him for that. She promised herself at that very moment that one day she would have record-breaking royalty statements and he would be sorry he had said that. "Well, I guess you could say I am. But let's talk about the novel, shall we?"

The waiter delivered a quart bottle of designer water to the table. Kate steeled herself and then began to pitch him the plot of her novel, *Decades,* a mother-daughter saga. Halfway through her three-minute synopsis, he interrupted her.

"I've heard a million stories like that, Kate. I'm sorry. Have you got anything else on the shelf? How about biographies—something with some scandal of Palm Beach old money?"

"What do you mean? I write fiction."

Rothstein shrugged his narrow shoulders. "Maybe. Look, I'm interested in your Palm Beach connections, but I have to see something more than columns."

"I have something—no one else has seen it." The lie came easily, as they always did, and Kate knew instantly how she would proceed.

For the first time, the man actually concentrated on her. "Send it in. I'll take a look." He glanced at his watch, put down a twenty-dollar bill to pay for the water, and got up. "Sorry, I've got to run."

They said good-bye on the sidewalk in front of the restaurant. His handshake was weak and as absentminded as his smile. "How long will it take you to look at the material?" Kate asked.

"Eight weeks, ten. Don't worry. And don't call me. You'll only frustrate yourself. Just be patient."

She pretended to hail a cab until he turned the corner, then she looked for the nearest subway. It might be quite some time before she had the money for taxicabs.

Kate and Lisa holed themselves up in the apartment for ten days. They worked at the magazine during the day, and at night, Lisa put her message machine on and let her own deadline slip. Kate told her she would give her 50 percent of the advance and a byline if the book sold. With Kate supplying the facts, Lisa threw together a proposal on the story of a politician's son who had been found dead of an overdose in the Peruvian Palace Hotel in Houston. Kate had not been interested in the story but she had stumbled on a lot of information concerning the subsequent cover-up. The material definitely fell into the area of celebrity biography, which was, as Lisa told her, Rothstein's bailiwick. It was Lisa who suggested they not tell Rothstein of her involvement until after he sold it.

"Just land the deal," Lisa advised her soon-to-be former roommate. "Once he's got the money on the table, he won't care who wrote it."

After that, there was nothing for Kate to do but return to Palm Beach and wait. And finish snaring Garrison.

Kate twirled in front of the mirror and smiled to herself. She had started to emphasize her resemblance to Christine, by slicking back her blonde hair, wearing the same makeup, and dressing in black. She was happy to have a friend who was so sophisticated, and surprised because she had always distrusted the companionship of women. However, she was flattered by Christine's open devotion to her. Christine wouldn't be there tonight, of course, but the two of them would have a ball gossiping tomorrow.

Garrison's chauffeur picked her up, and Kate gazed out of the limousine as they approached her destination. The trees loomed alongside the property, as tall as dark giants. There was only the sound of the car drawing up on the gravel drive. The butler opened the front door. The front hall was a blaze of orchids, roses, and lilies. As she entered the large drawing room, a uniformed maid offered champagne, sparkling in thin-stemmed glasses on a silver tray.

And then she saw Garrison. The color of his skin blended with the chestnut brown of his hair. He was standing back against a wall, aware of all the people, yet indifferent to them. She was about to go to him when she noticed that everyone's attention was fixed on the doorway. She turned.

Mrs. Morton entered in a whirl of raspberry silk. She had an air of a person who expects people to curtsy to her, Kate thought. People moved in circles around her, as if trying to acquire a suntan by means of an occasional ray, their smiles pleading to be acknowledged. Kate stared at her long bright red fingernails, her jewels, her hair. She was a daunting figure, Kate had to admit.

"Good evening."

She turned, then smiled at Garrison. "Good evening."

"Mother, you remember Kate," Garrison said, as his mother approached and kissed her son.

"Why, of course . . ." she said, extending her hand. "How nice of you to join us. . . ." Her words had the faint coating of mockery.

"How much longer will you be staying in Palm Beach, Miss Robinson?"

"Indefinitely, I think," Kate answered evenly. "I plan to finish a book I'm working on from here. As a matter of fact, I was so disappointed I couldn't join your son in Egypt a few weeks ago . . . but I must watch my deadlines." Mrs. Morton looked at Kate, who answered her gaze with an icy, triumphant stare.

Kate saw the dangerous flicker in the older woman's eyes, the warning, and looked away. As did Helen Morton. . . .

Garrison and she had had an argument an hour before the party. It had been over Kate. She had made it clear to her son that Kate was not welcome in her home. She wanted her son by her side to help her with the grueling series of social obligations of the season; she did not want him to bring along a girl. Especially this girl.

Helen Morton had taken an instant dislike to Kate. She was offended by what she instinctively sensed to be her fortune-hunting vulgarity. Garrison had insisted Kate was "a fine person," and that he would invite whom he wanted wherever he wanted. The matter of Kate Robinson was now a burden.

Unknown to the other, both women had drawn a mental picture of the other's face and classified it under the heading: *Enemy.*

"Well, I must attend to my other guests," Helen Morton stated. "By the way, where did you have your Valentino copy made?"

Kate blanched. She searched her mind for some retort to throw in Mrs. Morton's face, but she couldn't immediately think of anything...then it struck her. She flashed a wounded look at Garrison.

"I'm afraid I can't afford a real one," she said without embarrassment.

Kate had seen the ideal opportunity to cement her relationship with Garrison and seized it. She knew that he was now tempted to go in the complete opposite direction of what his mother wanted. It was perfect.

"Let's get out of here," said Garrison, giving his mother a look of steely disgust and firmly gripping Kate's hand.

The two walked in silence over to the guest house. Inside, he touched her face lightly before he kissed her. It was less a kiss of sexual desire than a kiss of a relationship, a beginning.

CHAPTER 12

$\mathcal{E}$urope was getting to be a drag and Sarah was ready to move on again. She had dropped out of Vassar immediately after the "accident" and run to London where she knew she could stay with her old flame, Victor Harold. That was three years ago, and Sarah rationalized that the reason much of the time seemed a blank was because it was so boring, though probably the drugs made her forget a lot of stuff—like some of her more ridiculous behavior.

She had actually been happy to leave school. She managed never to think about what happened in Poughkeepsie and she would have been successful in totally wiping the incident out of her mind except for the fact that Mother had cut off her allowance. Sarah was horrified at the thought of giving up her comfortable lifestyle and the possessions she enjoyed. She loved the taste, the feel, the smell of wealth. However, there was another intriguing aspect to her personality—as much as she loved having money, she loved divesting herself of it even more. Getting it, spending it—that was all that mattered. But now she had only her tiny trust fund, two thousand dollars a month, which to her meant she could barely eke out an existence. Clothes were expensive. Discos were expensive. Drugs cost more every day. Once in a while she was tempted to barter sex for coke but she managed always to get it some other way, at least so far.

Her bank account was closely supervised by a trust officer and her mother's accountant, and she was never allowed to borrow against it, no matter the circumstances. Invariably her account was empty by the end of the month as she continued to party and enjoy a life of reckless frivolity.

When she met Victor at a mixer he told her he had a job waiting for him as a lead guitarist in a great band. But the Deformities turned out to be a poor excuse for a heavy-metal threesome without even so much as a synthesizer. For a while it had been fun to roam around Liverpool with the other girlfriends, pretending that any minute the Deformities would be discovered like the Twisted Sisters, but it was clear to Sarah in the first six months that the band was going nowhere—and not even fast.

The whole group of them, but particularly Sarah, were known around London for their outrageous public behavior, especially when they'd been drugging. Even though she and Victor lived together, Sarah had a reputation for carrying on in bizarre ways. She had been photographed by a smart member of the paparazzi who didn't know her name but felt her practically naked body on the dance floor of Adelaide's was newsworthy. The photo had been picked up by one of the tabloids and it didn't take long before word got back to her mother who threatened to cut off even her trust fund. Sarah had no alternative but to leave London, which didn't seem like such a bad idea anyway, since not only was it becoming boring but Victor was hassling her to get work or do something to help pay expenses. The last thing she needed was someone else breathing down her neck.

Which is how she ended up in Amsterdam. But this was definitely not turning out the way she planned. The red light district was tawdry, not fun, and they didn't hire dancers, as she thought, just hookers, which she most certainly wasn't. The coffee houses sold only pot, and it was hard to get coke —only heroin seemed available on the street and Sarah wasn't interested. The addicts were eating the whole country alive and seeing them sleeping in the town squares frightened her—their rootlessness seemed too close for comfort.

She glanced to the sidewalk outside the cafe where a girl in tight hot pants was being offered by the man standing with her. Sarah looked into the prostitute's eyes and she saw a reflection of her own scared loneliness. Worse than being lonely, she was broke. She had chatted up a group of American students last night at this same coffee house and learned that it was impossible for an American to get work here— the Amsterdam government looked out for their own young people first, and Sarah would not get a job even if she wanted one and even if there was something she knew how to do.

She didn't notice the young blonde man until he sat down

at her table and spoke to her in a language she only recognized as Dutch. She didn't understand a word. But he was pointing at the hooker and the man with her.

"I'm sorry," she said. "I speak no Dutch."

"Do you care to?"

Sarah shrugged her shoulders. "I'm sorry," she repeated. I don't understand."

It was cold in the June night air and the canal sent a sort of damp pall over the whole country. She'd been here since last Thursday, and it had rained every single day. She had waited in the rain for everything, including two hours in front of Anne Frank's house, because she knew it was something she had to do if she were ever to go to heaven, even if God would forgive her for the accident. Which she wasn't sure He would—but there was still reason to try.

The blonde man was handsome in a sort of asexual way. She smiled at him tentatively. He managed somehow to get the waiter though Sarah had been waiting twenty-five minutes without success. He ordered something for them—beer she thought. And he offered her a cigarette from his pack. Unfiltered. She shook her head no.

"Are you American?" Oh thank goodness he spoke English. Maybe he'd buy dinner so the night wouldn't be a total loss. She was starving and her money was really low. Her trust fund was down to the nubs and it was not even the third week of June.

"Oh, great, you speak English."

"Yes, a bit. I have worked there."

"Where? In America?"

"Yes. And other places." The man's eyes followed the prostitute again and then he introduced himself. "I am Lauren."

"I am Sarah."

"So, you are sitting here alone. I think perhaps you long for some company. You want to join them?" This time when he nodded in the direction of the hooker and her pimp, Sarah got the message. Just then the waiter brought the beers. Too bad, Sarah thought, as she got up to leave. It was definitely time to go home.

———

Aspen, Colorado, wasn't home, but she felt welcome here. The ski community was just beginning to emerge as the playground for the idle rich and that was familiar ground. The party scene was rampant, and it hadn't taken her more than three days to get connected again. Now she knew where the best crowd could be found making their plans at dusk for the night ahead.

Sarah desperately needed to find work. How could it come to this? she asked herself. She had assumed that she would always be provided for, even after Daddy was gone. She was totally unequipped to earn a living. Something had to turn up—and soon.

Sarah was consoled by the fact that the two Fabrikant twins who she knew from prep school had offered her a place to stay until she got settled. They were not quite "our kind" and had always wanted to fit in with Sarah's crowd. It didn't matter. Sarah liked them, and more than that, liked being back in the party crowd. Still, neither girl worked, since their parents totally supported them, and last night at dinner it had been painful to see them throw their credit card on the table without a thought to who was going to pay the bill. Why oh why had she offered to buy tonight? What would happen when her credit card was rejected? Sarah broke out in a sweat just thinking about it. It seemed all she thought about was how to pay bills and how to get a place to stay while still appearing nonchalant. How had her life become so meaningless, so bland?

The restaurant was deceptively sparse. The light oak tables and bleached wood floor belied the pricey menu. Each girl ordered a vodka martini, Stolichnaya Cristal. Sarah couldn't look at the menu. Thankfully she still had a little coke left and so she wasn't hungry. Let the twins eat; neither of them did drugs. She would drink until the check came. And then she'd wing it.

The blonde man who waved to Barbara was handsome in a rugged sort of way. "Who's that?"

"Oh, that's Rob," Bonnie answered. "He's head instructor at Ajax."

Sarah had just come back from the ladies' room and she was feeling giddy. "Ask him to join us."

"Are you sure? I mean, we haven't, you know, he's not the most scintillating company, if you know what I mean," Barbara pointed to her head. "He's great on the slopes, but in the brain department, he's no bargain."

"That's okay. I like the way he looks," Sarah said and Bonnie waved him over.

The guy was quiet and his presence gave Sarah some respite from the nonstop chatter the twins seemed able to engage in on any subject, particularly if it was shallow. She allowed the others to talk among themselves and excused herself to go the ladies' room. When she emerged, the guy had ordered an appetizer and a bottle of champagne.

The bill was getting higher every time she turned around. She tried to figure out how much it would be, but the numbers kept slipping away and she had no idea how she was going to deal with this little problem—or any problem for that matter.

Barbara waved her over, and before Sarah could even sit down, the man poured her a glass of champagne. "You lovely women are celebrating on me tonight," he said, with a big proud smile on his face. "Where I come from, we don't get to entertain women like yourselves."

"Oh, and where do you come from?" Sarah turned up the volume on her smile. She knew that she could get him right where she wanted him. At this moment, Rob seemed like Prince Charming, smart or not. He had bailed her out without knowing it. Or maybe he did know it. And that made her smile even brighter.

After years of living a sordid city life it felt great to get in touch with her physical self, and Aspen offered opportunity with its risk-all-or-die philosophy about the outdoors. People skied here on breakneck slopes and some even risked climbing the sides of huge mountains with only rope, hooks, and sneakers. Rob was careful not to let her meet any of his friends. "They aren't good enough for you," he would say, since she had made it a point to tell him all about her pedigree that first night. With Rob's help, Sarah got back on the slopes after years and years of not skiing. The rush down the slick icy mountain to the spring green below reminded her of a happier time of life. She actually seemed to recall ski weekends in Vermont, even in Lausanne. And while these weekends with her father were mostly fabricated to impress, that didn't really matter, since Sarah half believed her own stories anyway. And Rob was impressed enough to hire her to teach beginners at the ski resort where he was head instructor.

But before too long the drug and party scene beckoned to

her. One weekend Rob had to leave town to take care of family business back in Seattle and she met a small-time drug dealer who was making Aspen his base for spring. By the time Rob returned, she was involved with the dealer, whose name was Cooper, or Coop as she called him. At first, she maintained the status quo with Rob, seeing him every day on the job and then pretending she was tired at night from all the activity. Then she'd slip out to go from party to party to see Coop, which is how he sold his drugs. But she couldn't keep it up. It was too difficult for her to juggle both men; it was only a matter of time before they found out about each other. And she couldn't maintain the discipline it took to get up early each day and face the mountains. So she quit the job—and Rob.

Coop worked from party to party, now always with Sarah at his side. He was discreet and generous with his drugs, and he took care of her habit. The truth was she was starting to feel a little out of control about the drugs—maybe a lot out of control. Sometimes she couldn't remember if she had just taken a hit or not and would find herself doing a line without realizing she had gone through the mechanics—the straw, the line, the cut. It was a little scary. She was hooked and there was no living without the white powder. Thankfully, Coop had plenty all the time.

More than the drug, she was hooked on the danger that was hinted at with each part of every deal. There was always the thrill of knowing any one of the suppliers could get nasty, or that clients might turn informer if they were caught. The risk was its own lure for Sarah. She knew that the party tonight was pretty hairy. The guy running it was new in town and Coop kept saying he had a strange vibration, but Sarah had convinced him to go through with it. "You worry too much," she said, knowing he liked her to think he had nerves of steel. She teased his mouth with tiny little kisses, and just as her hand went to his belt, he agreed to go through with it.

The party was hot and not only because a fireplace raged in the corner of the duplex condo. This crowd must be infiltrating from another hot spot—Tahoe maybe, or even Mont Tremblant in Montreal, she thought. The guys all had that Canadian look actually. They were big, rugged, not really skiers' bodies at all. More like professional athletes, football players. Or cops.

That thought occurred to her as she sat behind Coop and watched the negotiation going on. A leather suitcase filled with money was open on the glass and chrome table and the chairs and couches were all low-slung. Sarah felt defenseless, sitting back in the padded chair. She had gotten high back at Coop's place and her limbs seemed melted into the upholstery of the chair. The fire blazed behind her and sweat started to roll between her breasts. It was too hot for the nylon ski pants she wore. She should have changed into jeans and a denim shirt, like all the guys were wearing. And her cowboy boots would have been a better idea than the après-ski fur shorties. God, she was hot. And her heart had started to pound. She wondered if there was a graceful way to disappear for a second to take a hit.

Joe, who seemed to be in charge of the negotiations, had told them ahead of time that the women would come later, after the deal was done. Coop was talking real fast. He kept repeating he wanted to get business over with before the women arrived at eight o'clock. His foot was bouncing up and down and Sarah realized he was high. That was unlike Coop, who never mixed business with pleasure and hardly did coke at all. Maybe she shouldn't have encouraged him to get high before they came. The truth was she hadn't been the greatest influence on him.

That made her feel crummy about herself. After all, Coop had always been there for her. What was wrong with her anyway. She was turning into the scourge that her mother said she was—a shame, a black mark on the family's white linen history. Sarah maneuvered her body out of the chair and asked to be directed to the bathroom.

"Down the hall, to the right, second door," Joe said, without looking up.

This deal was making her a little too nervous. Everyone was so intense and the fun aspect of the danger cocktail she liked was lacking.

When she returned, Joe said, "You have powder on your nose." The suitcase was now on Coop's side of the table. This was the part where they went back to the car for the drugs. Except now "Joe" pulled a gun from somewhere and announced that he was DEA—Sarah couldn't believe that they actually handcuffed her.

She had to get out of Aspen. The bail was not her problem; let the sleazy bondsman come and find her—just let him try. She had to get out of here before her mother got wind of it or she'd be in real trouble. Too bad she couldn't get a message to Coop, but he hadn't made bail yet and she couldn't wait around. She had to fly.

Once out of the small jail where prisoners were kept overnight, Sarah quickly ran through her list of possibilities. Not enough money for a plane ticket, no more credit, couldn't rent a car without credit. She called the twins who had Merry Waltham, another old prep school friend, staying with them. Merry was driving home to Palm Beach tomorrow. Right then and there Sarah came up with a plan. She realized that the only thing that might make her mother soften a bit and free up some money was if she proved to be an embarrassment in front of the family's Palm Beach friends. But this time it wouldn't be embarrassment caused by her wild behavior, Sarah determined. This time it would be the humiliation of having her child not living well, properly, as dictated by their "class." Sarah was looking forward to it.

CHAPTER 13

Sarah hated the exhausting trip. Her frequent visits to the gas station bathrooms, which were pit stops only for quick hits of cocaine, were beginning to have their effects. She ate almost nothing, weighed almost nothing, and blew her nose frequently, feigning a cold. She did not want to share with Merry the tiny bit of coke she had left from the stash she lifted from Coop before she left. Her eyes were tired, and when she looked in the mirrors of the gas station rest rooms, she saw puffy pouches under them from too much drinking and too little sleep. She looked much older than twenty-three.

After five monotonous days of driving, at last they made it to Palm Beach. The first night she stayed with Merry, who was nice enough to invite her again the next night. But by the third night, Sarah wanted privacy. Merry's parents were rigorous about social conventions and it was tiresome to do and say the right things all the time. But she did score some points when she told them that her money was running low and she "couldn't seem to get Mother's accountant on the phone." That raised a few eyebrows, she was happy to see. Mr. Waltham offered to lend her a few hundred dollars to see her through, but Sarah, very cannily, declined. Why borrow a few hundred dollars when she was scheming to get her fortune back?

She moved into the Colony Hotel, getting a discount rate because of her name, and of course, there was no question about every item from moisturizing cream to steak tartare going on her long tab. Over Bloody Marys at the pool, she made the acquaintance of Kate Robinson and the two became fast friends. The journalist was amusing to listen to and seemed to have a somewhat detached perspective on the Palm Beach crowd. Enough so that Sarah could appreciate their foibles. And Kate knew her way around, not only the old guard, which was Sarah's family's stalking ground, but some of the newer-monied people as well. It was Kate who told her about the furnished room she knew was available for a rent Sarah could easily afford even on her meager trust fund.

Several Palm Beachers who knew Sarah's family gave parties for her the first few weeks, and she had sweet-talked Merry's father, who was on the board of the Everglades Club, into getting her a job in the tennis shop. She heard through the grapevine that her mother was quietly distraught at the idea of her daughter moving to Palm Beach, but Sarah was comfortable here. To her, Palm Beach was one of the most glamorous, beautiful towns in the United States, with an undercurrent of decadence that she liked.

But now, after only two months, Sarah was bored. The town of Palm Beach was exactly that—a town, without much action for young people. Her only activity seemed to be helping women members in their relentless search for the one tennis outfit that would do justice to their thighs (or conceal them, depending on the circumstances). The person whose company Sarah really enjoyed the most was Allison, the little girl whose mother worked near the club at the art gallery on Worth Avenue. Allison came to the club often to watch the members play. She reminded Sarah of a little puppy dog with her tongue hanging out at the butcher's window.

The time away from the Everglades was filled with partying, going to movies alone, since her one friend, Kate, was always busy covering the social scene, and reading everything she could get her hands on. The reading seemed to be the one good holdover left from Vassar. Kate always had great magazines and books laying around and was generous about lending them.

And Sarah played a lot of tennis, which is where she was going right now. The shop was closed in the middle of the day and the courts were available to employees when they were empty. It was much too hot to play in the middle of the afternoon except for the best players or those in great physical shape, which Sarah still was despite all the drugs. She picked up an uninspired game of doubles. Her game was getting pretty good and she was hoping to improve it enough to qualify as an instructor. She figured she could always use Rob's name as a reference. Poor Rob. Sometimes she missed the big lummox. But Aspen was history, along with the bail she'd run out on.

She returned to the shop until closing time and then went back to her little furnished room to spend yet another night alone.

There was a folded plastic sandwich bag next to Sarah's bed with a small mirror, razor blades, and a gold coke spoon. She carefully spooned a portion of the last of the white powder onto the surface, and with the blade, formed two lines. Sarah placed a straw up her right nostril, pressing the other nostril shut. She tilted her head back ecstatically. She would have to find herself a rich eligible to dally with. She was almost out of cocaine and money. It was time to make her move on Alfred Blum. She had met him at Merry's house. She loved the aura of power he exuded. Like many people of high birth, she had never known *great* money, so she was fascinated with Alfred's extreme wealth. He would be her prey.

Young as she was, Sarah knew from observing her family's friends over the years that every individual has three lives: a private life, a public life, and a secret life. What was Alfred Blum's secret? Where did his money come from? Her mother always said there are only two types of wealth— those who inherit it and those who marry it. Since her mother had taken her inheritance from her, Sarah would have to have a plan, because her life at the present was like her immediate past . . . intolerable. Even though she was not beautiful like her mother, she was extremely attractive and could be a charming and intelligent conversationalist. She had the unique knack of bringing up the right subject at the right time, and then entertaining the person on that subject.

She would have to go work on Blum. She had made serious mistakes in her past, and though they had not yet caught up to her, it was only a question of time before something else serious happened to her if she didn't find some way or someone to take care of her and fill the void in her life left when her father died. Palm Beach might just be her last chance to bury the past and forge a future. It was going to take money—lots of money—and Sarah didn't care where it came from.

Part Two
1990

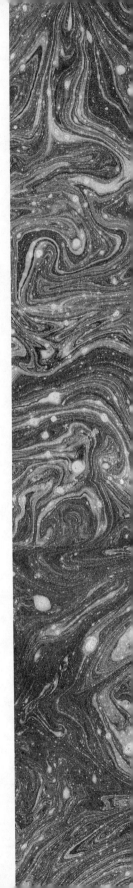

CHAPTER 14

$\mathcal{M}$aria sat at her desk. She had been through a very difficult day trying to answer letters, aiding one person on unjust imprisonment, locating the body of a drowned child in California, advising someone on whom to marry. As usual, she managed to answer personally only a small number of letters, sensing which cases most needed her help, always giving priority to her police cases. Now it was time for her to relax. She had just made herself a pot of tea.

Maria thought about her day, the people who had come in and out of her house. She had to work to keep down the flow of impressions, so she could somewhat enjoy normal relationships without seeing too much. She could pick up moods and thoughts of those around her, both in direct impression and in sensing their aura.

Her efforts to find a "normal" niche in modern society had never quite worked out. She had a failed marriage and no children, because work was her life. Maria never explained her abilities; she really couldn't. She merely saw herself as a person with a job to do, like other people with other talents. She knew she had an ability, and that at times it was a remarkably good one.

She had learned early in life that her gift for "insight" functioned best when she stuck close to her own religious affinities. After reading the Bible, praying, and meditating, disciplines that she still undertook daily, she could be more accurate and detailed with her insights. As long as she tried to help others more than herself, and if she achieved purity of heart toward them, she could expect to find her psychic stream overflowing, and then, more often than not, she was supplied with whatever was needed for the particular situation from the Giver of all good.

Maria was conscious never to coast on the achievements of this life or a past life, or to slide into narcissism, or be buried by a concern for power or position. Her greatest pleasure came from helping people help themselves. It was never her intention to try to convert anyone to her own beliefs; however, when people came to her for advice, she would try to look into their karma, which she knew was the Sanskrit word for "action." She would explain to them that karma is merely a process of evolution, of achieving a greater level of perfection, an opportunity to make new decisions and choices. The soul always has free will, the freedom of choice. The purpose of karma is not to punish but to purify. The laws of karma are perfectly just. It is the perfect memory bank.

She would always tell them that everybody has some measure of psychic ability—hunches, premonitions, intuition; the degree depended on the person's awareness of this ability. These natural happenings were available to every soul whose life was not so cluttered with defenses and guilts as to block the flow of positive energies. So when people came to her, she would look into their karmic cycle in an attempt to help people understand why they do what they do, and show them how to avoid making the same mistakes over and over.

The sound of a heartbeat suddenly filled the room. Who was in danger? The question pounded against her skull with a rhythm. Then she caught several impressions, one after the other, of the four friends. She immediately pulled out her deck of cards and took the Queen of Clubs from the pack.

Christine Wells had been married to Lawton Dodd for several years now, and they had a daughter. Maria smiled to herself as the wave of Christine's satisfaction over her social position swept through her body. But there were problems here . . . financial problems . . . was it blackmail? Marie was trying to look deeper into Christine's karmic cycle. There was much disappointment and heartache in her closest relationships. Maria liked her. She was always positive and had a strong will, but when suffering came, it was deep and lasting.

She pulled out the Queen of Hearts.

Maria did not particularly like Kate Robinson. She scolded herself for letting that dark thought enter her mind. Honestly sought, the flow of love could be found in anyone, for anyone. Maria knew she was not a saint, and that she had her

temper, her moods, but she had to ignore her personal feelings now. Was Kate in danger? She concentrated. Kate had
been in with the other girls a few weeks earlier for a reading.
Maria knew she was only using her as a psychic character
for her next book. And Maria had gotten short and impatient
with Kate's manipulative attitude, suggesting she do some
thinking for herself for a change.

Kate had married Garrison Morton. She was on the verge
of becoming a best-selling author. But there was betrayal
and deceit here...deceit over her work...deceit over
promise of a child. Disappointment through failure to attain
a cherished objective. Is there not sufficient talent? Maria
wondered.

Maria wished Kate could see that one only has himself to
blame or credit for his life. One can only fool himself tem-
porarily.

Maria's head jerked slightly. She was interrupted by new
impressions...a man's...

The strides were long and quick and stopped at Maria's
door. Gus Smith stood with one hand in his pocket, the other
holding a cigarette. Deep lines jutted out from the corners of
his eyes, the result more of squinting against the glare of a
tropical sun than of age, although five decades had come and
gone. He rang the doorbell for Maria.

Maria...always gentle, yet direct. Many people believed
she had changed their lives when all seemed lost. She certainly had helped him on numerous occasions. One time she
told him his son needed a cancer specialist, diagnosing the
disease before any symptoms had shown up. To him, she
displayed powers of perception that seemed to extend far
beyond the normal range of the five senses. Yet Maria never
publicized her abilities or made claim about them. She never

sought money. The absence of greed puzzled Gus almost as much as the subject of parapsychology itself. Her house held hidden secrets and psychic mysteries. All he knew was that once he got inside, there was such deep peace, a field of goodness that seemed to build up around her so that he never wanted to leave.

Maria opened the door and smiled at Detective Gus Smith. The two walked immediately to her study.

"I need your help," he stated.

Maria stared at the piece of paper he put down on her desk:

VICTIM: *Karen Biven*
DOB: *6/21/76*
AUTOPSY RESULTS: *Death by knife wound to right side, piercing heart*
DIAMETER: *⅛"*
SPERM ANALYSIS: *Type A positive*

Gus stared at the wall behind her desk, which was solid books.

"Anything else?" she asked.

Gus brought out a knife from his pocket, clicked it open. It had been wiped clean when he found it. The blade was long, thin, very sharp. He handed it to Maria.

Sometimes Maria needed only to be given something owned by the suspect and she would be able to tune in telepathically to that individual's mind and body. Gus hoped that was the case now.

Over the years, he had received help from Maria locating

murder suspects, which had proved incredibly accurate and detailed, yet when she missed and it cost someone a life, the pain was devastating.

Maria now held the knife, and staring at it, she knew there was hope for the case.

"He is in Florida," she began. "Miami . . ."

She began to perspire heavily. "The palm trees on the street have just had all the coconuts cut down. . . . There are huge piles of palm fronds on the south side of the property."

Suddenly a sucking noise started in the back of her throat, and her hands flew dramatically to her heart.

"136 Bent Cypress Road."

There was silence. Minutes passed, and then she got to her feet, began to pace the floor to cool down, as she always did after intense concentration.

"You okay?" Gus asked, weak with amazement, as always after a session with her.

"Let me know, Gus."

"I will," he promised, the knife clasped tightly in his hand as he left.

Maria sipped the cold tea. She felt drained, yet she knew she had to go back to the four young women. The common source of their pain was the betrayal by those they loved the most.

She pulled out the Queen of Spades.

Jessie had been having an affair with Ned for years.

A married man. Maria had counseled her, consoled her, and advised her often enough—but now Maria felt the guilt.

Oh, how she loved Jessie. She was like the daughter Maria never had.

Yet, such sadness. . . . She had come to the world to lead and direct, but found herself in a subordinate position. Jessie knew, deep inside, she did not belong here. She didn't want to be held "down to earth." She was struggling to get back where she belonged; however, she didn't know how to do that.

Maria suddenly felt cold tile against bare feet. It was danger. Allison was in trouble. Maria *never* looked in the cards about people's children. It was her rule.

The Queen of Spades would not talk further. Maria got nothing.

The Queen of Diamonds was pregnant. Sarah didn't even know it herself. Two men will think they are the father. An arrest . . . handcuffs. Money. Money, money.

Maria shook her head.

Money will not buy happiness for a person who has no concept of what he truly wants. Money will not give one a code of values if you have evaded the knowledge of what to value. Money will not provide one with a purpose if you have evaded the choice of what to seek.

This girl was born with an all-absorbing money consciousness from her first breath.

Overdose?

Maria stared at the four Queens. Each of these girls, souls created in the beginning, each with its own unique design, as delightful and original as a snowflake.

What worried her was the reaction of these girls in the individual tests of their lives—the negating of hatred, revenge, jealousy, fears. If they do not learn their lessons, they will have to retake the tests in either this lifetime or a future one.

Karma would require much courage for these girls to face

their shortcomings, and even more courage to do something constructive about them.

Maria could only help if the student was ready. Not one of them sensed the danger.

The water, no air, the dark, struggling. The sight of a body hit Maria with the abruptness of a collision. The King of Spades . . .

Maria fought back the panic.

Why wasn't she being given all the answers? How could she help? She pursed her lips and waited. Nothing.

She slumped back, exhausted. She was trying to force rather than wait for it to be given. Perhaps the fault was hers. She knew she was supposed to keep a distance from the problems and the personalities.

But how could she when she saw that for someone close to her . . . a heart would stop.

CHAPTER 15

*W*hat a glorious day, Christine mused, as she and Lawton walked up the church's front steps. She lifted her chin proudly, her beautiful blonde hair flowing in the gentle breeze. Sunday Mass was the only time Christine was not dressed in her "trademark" black. This Sunday she was wearing a yellow dress.

Looking back, Christine realized how hard she had fought for the privilege of worshipping at Bethesda by the Sea, which was attended by only the most proper Palm Beach Episcopalians. How ironic, since now her husband wanted to leave it. Outsiders in general had to worship off the island, in West Palm. Catholics, even Kennedys, were not welcome here. So why was Lawton pressing her to leave this congregation?

The pastor droned on, serving as background noise for Christine's private reflection. So much has happened over the past several years. She and Lawton had been married four years ago and now there was Alexandra, a lovely ten-month-old baby girl; her business was successful. And thanks to Lawton's prodding, she was a contributing member to several charity and society organizations. She managed all her roles quite well. But the most important was her role as Mrs. Dodd, wife to Lawton and a sterling member of Palm Beach Society.

The day they were married, Lawton had provided her with a list of the people he expected her to associate with in order to establish them as a couple. With his patient tutoring, she had learned to play hostess to a shimmering assortment of people she had once only read or heard about—or watched from afar. Lawton had hired them a publicist to orchestrate behind the scenes his own rise to prominence as banker to society. And also, to push them as a couple to the forefront of society's scene. He had relied on her connection to Alfred to make it into the offices of Palm Beach elite, both old money and new. In fact, just a few weeks ago Kate Robinson had published a piece on him as Palm Beach's Favorite Banker.

Christine had made her role as Lawton's wife her priority. She had hired a manager to run Seasons, which was entirely hers now, Alfred having been paid back, at least in terms of money. The rest would come in time. And he had been beneficial to Lawton, which was all that mattered to her.

Next to her, Lawton sang the closing hymn along with the

congregation. It would be impossible for anyone to tell that her husband was going through some sort of a transformation. Who would have guessed that the man sitting next to her was in the throes of what he called a spiritual crisis? Who would have thought a man like Lawton considered the spirit at all?

His handsome face always seemed to magnetize her, and now, Christine had to pull her eyes away to concentrate on the end of the service. Their life was promoted as perfect. Kate was not the only journalist who wrote pieces about their lifestyle in fashionable magazines. They were invited to all the right parties. Photographers waited for them wherever they went. They were seen everywhere, out every night. Christine Wells had made it up from the pits of despair to the elite. No longer did she feel like a foreigner. And having come this far, her social ambitions were even more ferocious. She wanted to stay in the proximity of these people who had a level of refinement she had once only admired. She loved to revel in the possibilities the future held for her and her beloved family. But now, Lawton threatened all of this with his newfound passion—

The service was ending and Christine had to pull herself back from a million miles away. Her husband's wide shoulders parted the crowd in front of her, and as always, she automatically checked his appearance in case a photographer should show up. Perfect—every hair in place, each crease in his trousers sharp. The only problem was that Mrs. Lawton Dodd wasn't quite sure what her husband was up to.

Although she was not expected to contribute money from the hotel's earnings to the marriage, lately she had been forced to—funds had been disappearing from their joint savings account.

"Darling, are you all right?" Lawton smiled at her, solicitous as always, but the smiles never seemed to reach his eyes anymore. "You seemed so far away in the service. Does that mean you're thinking it over?"

Christine didn't answer right away. Lawton had always been generous with his donations, but she had seen several checks in large amounts made out to something called the Assembly of God. When she asked him about it, he had snapped that she should mind her own business. Eventually he had relented and told her the money was going to Peru to help build a church for the poor. When she had been unable to hide her shock, he had glared angrily at her and stormed out—disappearing for two days. By the time he returned, she was so frantic, she would have allowed him anything—even the money for the Assembly of God.

Lawton had been good to her from the very beginning of their relationship. He had taught and guided her, never making fun if she committed some social gaffe. Though her "profession" in London had taught her how to get along with all kinds of people, Palm Beach society adhered to a code of behavior uniquely its own. Without Lawton, she never would have maneuvered her way through it. Gratitude drove her to please him more and more and it drove her now to say what she knew he was waiting to hear.

"Perhaps." She wasn't about to say more.

Somehow Lawton managed to find a quiet pocket in the crowd of admirers. "Say you'll think about it. Your support would mean so much to me, my darling."

What he wasn't saying was that if she didn't go along with his bizarre plan for the future, she wouldn't be Mrs. Dodd anymore.

"How are you, Mrs. Dodd?" Every Sunday it was the

same. A group of admirers, plus a few sycophants, would circle the Lawtons hoping for an invitation to their famous postservice lunch.

"I'm fine," she answered, on automatic, her smile pasted on while her thoughts went elsewhere. But she wasn't fine; things weren't fine anymore. They were fairly topsy-turvy.

Christine had tried to understand him. She respected her husband's reborn devotion to the church but she could not let him squander their fortune—her fortune—as well as their place in society. If he went ahead with his plan, they would be as poor as the people he was trying to help. And then they would slip out of society, which is what she feared. And what he kept saying he didn't care about. Really, it was too bizarre. He had worked so hard to get to the pinnacle they now occupied, and now he was planning a future that would force them to abandon it. She had to convince him that he could be a good Christian *as well as* a social lion.

As she watched, Lawton held out his hand to an older woman and passed the time of day with her. As always, Christine's heart melted as she saw how easily people were drawn to him. Her husband could talk to a complete stranger and make him feel like a close friend. She listened as he spoke with smooth, cheerful assurance about his opinion on that morning's sermon.

"Please join us for lunch," he invited the group around them. Then he walked off, completely sure of himself, and as pleased as if he had hit a beautiful golf stroke.

Christine turned to survey the magnificent flower arrangements that had been artfully dispersed throughout the house. She and Lawton had purchased a home on Seascape and she had seen to every detail of the decoration with her usual precision. The house was made to throw lavish parties and

Christine loved to entertain, giving and going to ten or even fifteen black-tie parties in a month. She enjoyed their life completely, and more so since she discovered that quite a few of the other prominent hostesses had managed to climb to the top from humble origins as well, although she didn't imagine any of them had begun as a whore.

Christine stared at her husband. Her past seemed light-years away. That old life was gone forever. She was now Mrs. Dodd. But how long would that mean what it did today?

She moved from guest to guest, enjoying herself. She was laughing gaily and seeing the smiles of response from her friends. She kept glancing at Lawton, radiantly, like a child handing him a report card with straight A's, begging him to be proud of her.

Lawton nodded back at her, knowing she relied on his approval. Society was entertained by his wife, and in the beginning he had been eager to display her. He had married her because she was beautiful, a sexual witch, and smart. Although his true sexual interest had always been men, he had, most of the time while he was married, successfully suppressed these tendencies . . . until lately.

He genuinely like Christine, but their life together was not enough. Nothing would ever be enough until he achieved what he realized now would give him true pleasure: power over people. Banking did not give him this, not really. His money and social standing did not give him this. And sex with an eager, willing boy did not give him this. It was from the pulpit, he had come to realize, that he would have the true mastery over people he craved. He enjoyed watching people smile for him, pleading to be noticed. No one could control the feelings of people as much as a priest. He had come to understand and want this for himself.

Lawton watched his wife walk around their living room as if she were born to be a social queen bee. She was getting admiration on her own now, not because she was his wife, on her own merit, as she did with the hotel. He felt irritation at the smooth efficiency she exuded. It was her poise that irritated him most now . . . in the beginning it had been what he admired most. Now she could end up being dangerous for his plans unless she went along. She wouldn't want him to leave his position. But he could handle her. He was not going to alter his course. . . .

"Enjoy this now, Christine," Lawton whispered in her ear. "In the future, we will be surrounded by a different group of people."

Christine said nothing. The party flowed around them as the couple stared each other down.

Where was the awe, the admiration he had expected from his wife?

"The church has asked me to accompany a group of delegates to Albania. Their newfound status leaves them more open to receiving us. We are to bring the Word to them. We're smuggling in Bibles."

Her eyes disturbed him now; they were neither friendly nor hostile, just watchful.

"Well? Do I have your support in this?"

"I don't understand why you would want to do that," she said finally.

"If you don't understand, I can't explain it to you." His tone implied that her lack of understanding was an admission of shameful inferiority. The color drained from his face. Mostly he was angry because she seemed to feel sorry for him.

"Hi . . . am I interrupting something?" asked Kate, coming into the room and going directly over to the couple.

"Well, well, don't you look absolutely gorgeous today," Lawton said, smiling and relieved to be able to change the subject.

"How are you, Lawton?" Kate said coldly. Everyone knew she hated Lawton, believing he was a complete phony. The key to his demented personality, she told people, including his wife, was that he only complimented his enemies.

Lawton knew Kate didn't like him, and the feeling was mutual. He thought the ex-New Yorker was almost a caricature of the "pushy broad" type. However, she was the godmother of his child, and Christine's best friend, so he was always courteous. But for the life of him, he couldn't picture the two as friends.

"Where's Garrison?" Christine asked.

"He's playing doubles at the club with the Winstons and Sarah. He said he might stop by, but you know Garrison. Don't hold your breath."

Lawton excused himself from the women to circulate among his "audience," as he viewed his guests. No sooner was he out of earshot than Christine turned to her friend and grasped her hand urgently.

"Oh, Kate," she began, her voice almost teary.

"Christine, what is it? What's wrong?"

"I've got a problem, Kate. A bad one. Alfred called yesterday afternoon. He wants to see me."

"So? He's your partner."

"More than that, Kate," Christine admitted in a whisper.

Over the past few years, Christine had poured out her heart to Kate, putting her trust in her about her past, about Ned, her father. She had never told her about Alfred, though. But then, a few months ago, she had covered for Kate when her friend had had a weekend fling with a reporter at the hotel. For some reason, knowing that about Kate helped her feel she could reveal the last secret about herself.

"It's not entirely business with Alfred, never has been," Christine confessed.

Kate's eyebrows rose with interest, but she said nothing, waiting for Christine to go on.

"Part of my original deal with him to get financing for the hotel was that I had to agree to sleep with him whenever he wanted. He knew about my life in England and thought he was just continuing with what I knew; he'd give me money and I'd perform, only this time the money went for the hotel."

"Is this still going on?" Kate asked.

Christine nodded miserably. She thought briefly of Alfred. To her, their sex life held neither joy nor sin. She was supposed to sleep with him so she did. It was an attitude that had helped her be such a successful courtesan years ago. It was an attitude that had helped her create a world for herself here in Palm Beach. Her getting married had stopped nothing, but now she felt a desperate need to break free of him. She needed to reestablish some control over her life. Lawton was clearly going crazy, draining their finances and throwing their future into disarray. Christine felt she might go mad right along with him if she didn't stop the world from its cockeyed spinning. Sex for pay with Alfred had turned from an innocuous bargain to a symbol of her precarious hold on this life she so cherished. She could not pretend that giving herself away meant nothing to her. She could not pretend that her relationship with Alfred meant nothing to her, just as she could not continue to hope that things would improve with Lawton. She had no control over these things. She had to do something, but what, what? Perhaps if she were finally able to free herself of Alfred, she would feel on top again. He had gotten more than he paid for, from her and the hotel.

"I've got to break it off with him, Kate," she said.

"But why now, after all this time?" Kate would never tell her friend, but she was thrilled with this new information. She had always wanted to get to Alfred. Now maybe she could.

"He was good to me when I needed it. I felt I owed him. But I can't keep doing it."

"Christine, you haven't answered me. Why can't you? What's different now than six months ago, two years ago?"

"It's Lawton—" Christine began, but before she could continue her husband was striding over to her, a smile on his face, his arm at the elbow of one of Palm Beach's premier dowagers.

———

Christine lay in bed, propped against pillows of pale pink linen. Her bed jacket was also pale pink satin, and she wore it with the pristine perfection of a mannequin. The night table held a novel, a glass of Evian, a Limoges bud vase with one white rose, and a Lalique lamp. The scene was a decorator's display of perfection.

"You didn't seem to be very impressed with my news this afternoon," Lawton said from the bathroom doorway. "It's a mission. A worthy public-spirited mission to help the underprivileged."

She merely sat looking at him without speaking.

"You couldn't possibly understand," he said suddenly.

"Then explain it to me, Lawton. Help me understand."

"You should care more. You should have more humanitarian instincts for the poor. You didn't come from wealth."

For Lawton's sake, Christine had manufactured a story about her past, making herself the child of a British bureaucrat, a man who served in the protocol office. And after a while, Australia and her life there grew farther and farther away until her parents were dead to her before they passed away. It was only Kate who knew everything, and perhaps Alfred, and Ned. . . . Sometimes Christine wondered how she kept her stories straight. But Lawton never doubted her story, or so he said. Perhaps he just didn't care.

"Lawton, I don't believe you care about the poor either. I'm not sure what your real motive is, but it's not charity."

"Well, you only care about your parties."

"That's not true."

"It doesn't matter. We're going to start attending the Assembly of God church where I can do some preaching." He stopped. He had slid too far. He had let a dangerous word slip out involuntarily.

"What?"

"I'm going to be bigger than Billy Graham. You'll see." There was a feverish sparkle in his eyes.

"You can't do that." She leaned back, away from his madness. He frightened her.

"Oh for Christ's sake!" he screamed. "Is this the gratitude I get?" His baritone voice was a seismic rumble echoing with the threat of upheaval, violence.

He came toward the bed, raising his hand.

Christine's shoulders sagged, and her face looked suddenly worn, and lost. That's what her father used to do when he got drunk. The memory was vague and fuzzy. One that she preferred to keep buried in the deep recesses of her mind. But now it appeared, all too vividly.

She could see her father's face. It was covered with shaving cream and he held a razor in one hand. He had been beaten as a child, and her mother had told her "his residual anger had to be taken out on his family." Her father could be very scary. He would give one long, cold stare, and everyone scrambled away as if they were playing musical chairs and the music had just stopped.

The last piece of Lawton's puzzle fell into place. Christine finally understood his plan. She felt herself slipping on the polish of the pillar she thought was her marriage.

The next day she met Alfred at their usual rendezvous location: her old suite of rooms at the hotel, now kept at the ready for any visiting dignitary.

Christine was not looking forward to this confrontation with her old partner. Even if he agreed to stop using his right to have sex with her, he would always be able to hold that over her head, a threat to the facade of propriety she had worked so arduously to attain. But there was nothing to be done about that. She would prefer to live with the threat than continue to have sex with him. The thought of what he could do to her was frightening; her hold on society was fragile, despite being married to Lawton. If Alfred chose, he could completely destroy her. But since her own husband seemed to be doing that, the risk Alfred posed didn't matter. She just wanted a semblance of control over her destiny.

As it turned out, Christine had little to worry about, never really had, Alfred told her. He had never expected her to keep up her end of the bargain once she had married Lawton, and certainly not after she had her child, but when he had, on a dare, called her for their regular session, and she had agreed, he assumed it was because she *enjoyed* it as much as he. No, there would never be any threat from him, now or in the future. He had invested wisely and felt he owed Christine quite as much as she owed him. It had all worked out well for both parties, and he hoped they could remain friends.

So it was that when Christine returned home later that afternoon, it was with a renewed sense of hope that things would straighten out between Lawton and herself as well. This new foolishness of his with the church and the poor would stop. She would find out what he really hoped to accomplish, and they would resume the happy existence they deserved.

CHAPTER 16

Once a month the four friends met for a game of doubles and sometimes also a reading afterward at Maria's. Christine and Kate were members of the Everglades, and Sarah still maintained employee privileges. Jessica usually arrived first, often with Allison who would go to the gallery after school. But today, Jessica was late. Sarah wasn't free until four. Kate was impatient. Her first book about the Peruvian Palace Hotel scandal had been moderately successful and she had been on deadline ever since, rushing from the first book to another, an unauthorized celebrity bio. The money was coming in, Eric Rothstein was pretty quick to answer her phone calls. . . .

And in a few weeks, her name would finally be on everybody's lips. Her third book was being published—finally,
the novel—and would be celebrated at a publishing party in
New York, which was a statement of her value; a symbol of
the publisher's belief in her success. Her life would be
crowded with publicity tours, including all the television,
radio, and print media. Kate would do whatever it took. She
just had to get on the *New York Times* best-seller list. But so
far, that had eluded her.

Lost in thought, Kate hardly noticed Christine warming
up. Her friend looked different, lighter than the day of the
luncheon.

"What's the matter, my little Christine, no black outfits in
the pro shop?"

It was a running joke between them. Christine was flattered by Kate's habit of always wearing black. She knew that
Kate's husband, Garrison, hated it. But that didn't stop Kate.
Nothing had stopped her, it seemed, since the first book
came out.

"Hey—let's hit a few while we wait. I feel glorious
today."

"Want to talk about it?"

"No, let's wait until we get to Maria's, okay? Suffice it to
say I feel free."

Interesting, Kate thought. That meant Blum was free.
Well, except for his wife, of course, but that situation was
clearly nearing an end, her sources told her. She kept tabs
on Blum these days through a former valet who had been
unjustly dismissed. Or had been dismissed for stealing, Kate
thought was more likely.

Sarah arrived looking a little peaked. Her days were frac-
tured, Kate knew. She had earned her tennis instructor's
certificate, and though not able to teach adults as a pro, she

did teach children in West Palm. At night, she partied. A lot. It was beginning to wear on her and not very well. None of them was getting any younger. Cripes, Kate figured Sarah must be pushing thirty.

Allison watched from the shade of a malacca tree. The Australian imports did well in the tropical climate. Behind the trees, Kate knew, there was a creek in which alligators lived and it amused her that every so often one of the giant lizards would crawl up onto the grounds and spook everyone.

Finally everyone was there. Christine and Kate played partners against Sarah and Jessica.

"Hey, Christine, want to stop figuring out your net worth for a minute and play tennis?" Christine was the least athletic, and Kate made constant jokes about it. Sarah felt a stab of jealousy. She hated the easy friendship between the two and never understood what Kate liked about Christine Wells. She was so aloof all the time. Just being around Christine made Sarah feel dirty, guilty, as though Christine's pure blue eyes could look past her veneer into her soul's dirty secrets. The fact that Christine had secrets of her own never occurred to Sarah.

The ball bounced on Jessica's side just at the net and she couldn't get there in time.

"Mother, pay attention!"

Kate shifted her attention to the child who was growing up right before their eyes. She figured Allison was nearly thirteen, maybe pushing fourteen. How could Jessica have a child that age? She was so innocent-looking. It was hard to believe she was involved with someone else's husband.

As though Christine had read her mind, she paused in the middle of her serve and searched Kate's face. Kate was the only one of the friends who knew Christine's past with Ned and only Kate would ever know. But Jessica and Ned were an open secret. Kate always wondered how Christine kept so cool about it. Must be the whore in her, Kate thought, without recrimination. They were all selling something of themselves in a way. Perhaps me most of all, Kate thought.

The group appointment at Maria's was something they had stumbled upon together. Jessica had been first; she was the one who actually believed in crystals and stones and miracles. She had brought the rest of them to Maria's.

At first, it had been a joke, a way to spend time together instead of tennis or the gym. Then Kate had still been writing her early pieces about the people of Palm Beach and she thought the psychic might add some local color. That brought her back a second time, though Maria had been quite snippy and withholding. Now they went as a team and Jessica would come by herself intermittently. Maria sat them around a table and soon even the dubious Kate would begin to feel a sort of flow happening among them.

Maria usually read cards to start. As she picked each card from the pack, she would seem to peer into it, and then a kind of eruption would issue from her, a torrent of thoughts that were more feeling than coherent sense.

"I don't like this today," Maria said, as her beautiful eyes welled up and Christine felt something grab at her insides. She was sorry she had come. She had been feeling so free after meeting with Alfred and now despair threatened to descend over her again. When she looked up from downcast eyes, she saw that Maria was looking straight at Jessica.

"I don't want to stay here for this," Sarah leapt up from the table. "I'm in a bad place today. I'll wait outside."

"No, come back. You can't run all the time," Maria said, but her words seemed to come from far away.

"Yes I can." Sarah slammed the door behind her. Kate knew she wouldn't go anywhere. Sarah didn't drive very well and she had seemed high on something. As long as Kate had known Sarah, she did not drive when she had been drugging.

Maria took the top four cards from the deck. All four Queens. As the three friends looked on helplessly, Maria began to cry.

CHAPTER 17

$\mathcal{K}$ate approached the mansion, regarding it as she always did, as if it were a living thing, a person, rather than a structure. Her steps were cautious, those of a child approaching a mean relative. The butler, Jason, greeted her in the front hall.

She looked around her mother-in-law's living room and thought how alike these Palm Beach homes were: flowers everywhere, all arranged by the decorator of the moment . . . baskets for magazines, photographs in silver frames, chintz . . . beautiful houses without true style or personality, all interchangeable. Kate didn't see the point in any of it. She hated these people, not for their material possessions, but because they had success from the moment they were born as a result of their background, not their accomplishments.

A shiver ran down her spine. She was so unsure of herself. She thought of the times she looked down at a blank piece of paper . . . and could find nothing to say. The long hours she spent trying. Then how she would always have to rush off to New York to visit her old roommate, Lisa, who helped her rewrite. She closed her eyes. The old feeling of not being good enough swept over her. As did the problems in her marriage.

She tried to piece it all together. The first few years they lived together had been relatively happy ones. He added a new wing onto the house for her, which became her study, understanding her desire to succeed.

Then, gradually, things changed. Perhaps it was Garrison's travels or her own single-mindedness to have a successful career. They didn't even make love very often anymore. Those nights were rare, widely spread in time, and only occurred after careful deliberation on her part. She had had a few affairs on the side, during her travels, but nothing important. She never concerned herself with her husband's life, how he spent his time, or with whom. If he had other women, she didn't know or care about them.

In the beginning, Garrison had been obsessed with having a child; it was all he talked about. But with a financially secure marriage, Kate felt free to concentrate on a career, not motherhood. So she had lied to him. In her teens, she had told him, she had had an abortion that caused her severe problems that plagued her still, so having a baby would be difficult. After that "confession," Garrison's need for sex with her dwindled as much as the time they spent together.

But Kate couldn't help it. She didn't want children or anything else she viewed as interference in her career, and that included a needy husband.

Where was her mother-in-law, Kate thought now, getting angry. She was the one who had requested this meeting. How she hated the woman. There had never been any pretending about that. Over the years, they had learned to put up with each other, but their mutual loathing was known to all. Among the many things Kate disliked about Helen Morton was the impersonal politeness she always had on her face when the two met in public. She resented that the most. Kate was very aware that Garrison had brought all the influence he had to bear in high society to counteract the opposition from his mother, but still, everyone knew that the two women in Garrison's life detested each other.

Kate, tired of waiting, walked into the master bedroom. "Hello? Helen?"

She glanced out the French doors. She could see two acres of lawn rolling down to the ocean. She stood for a moment gazing at the glimmering water. She turned, and spotted a framed picture of Garrison, as a child, on the bedside table. Next to it, lying open, was Mrs. Morton's diary.

Kate couldn't help herself. She read last night's entry. She stood there like a foreigner who recognized some of the words, but couldn't put them into sentences.

"Oh my God." She caught her breath, cutting off all but the faint echo of a gasp. She ripped out the page and put the diary back on the nighttable. On that page was the name of the man she, Kate, had slept with last week, when seeing Lisa in New York, and all the details. The damn bitch had a p.i. following her.

"What are you doing in here?" Mrs. Morton demanded,

cutting resolutely across the room, her voice taut and harsh. Kate's hand jerked like the withdrawal of a shoplifter's hand caught in action.

"You kept me waiting for over a half hour. You're the one who said it was imperative to talk to me."

"Yes, I wanted to tell you that I know all about your little affair last week with the photographer," Mrs. Morton began. The hint of a smile on her face had the sheen of gloating. "I know what you've been doing behind my son's back."

Kate was speechless and actually took a step back, as if she had been slapped.

"I would be happy to give you a little nest egg if you quietly get out of my son's life," the matriarch continued. She kept her voice smooth, but with a carefully measured hint of harshness. "Otherwise, I shall inform him of your infidelities. I'm going to protect him against you once and for all. You're nothing but a gold-digging phony who came here to Palm Beach to make something of yourself out of someone else's weaknesses. Well, you might have deceived my son, but you haven't fooled me for a minute, and now I'm going to make sure the blinders are taken off Garrison, too."

Kate pressed her lips together, making her mouth one razor-thin line. "You've been trying to destroy this marriage from the beginning, but you've only succeeded in driving your son farther away from you." And then Kate tapped her purse where she had hastily put the torn-out diary page. "You old fool! Tell your precious son anything against me, Mrs. Morton, and I promise you, it'll be you he runs from, not me. He'll think you made it all up. You and the people you have hired to help you. He's hated it from day one that you've never supported me. He'll never believe you against me, *never!*"

"Mother? What's going on?"

Mrs. Morton turned slowly at the sound of her son's voice. "Why, Garrison . . ." she began, he face totally lifeless like the skull of a skeleton. And then suddenly, her hand flew to her chest and her mouth opened wide in a silent scream as she collapsed to the floor, Kate standing by and watching her enemy die.

———

Garrison looked around at the streets of New York. He had just finished playing tennis at the New York Athletic Club and was on his way back to the St. Regis Hotel on Fifth and Fifty-fifth. He and Kate were here for her publication party, only weeks after the death of his mother.

Losing his mother had greatly distressed him. He pictured her now, dressed in black as usual, with ropes of pearls enveloping her long neck. The woman had very little to do with raising him; they had actually become closer after he had become an adult. He had spent more time with the soldier chauffeur and the English nanny. He wondered for a moment if he had ever really loved his mother. Still, she had been his mother; he had always simply taken it for granted that whatever he felt for her was love. If he were to be honest with himself, what he felt was more like his cordial affection for a distant aunt.

For all the immense privilege he had enjoyed as the winner of the biological lottery, he had felt lost, as a child, in the world of private beaches and tennis clubs, and houses that had been in the family since the beginning of the century. The thousands of dollars spent on parties, the society orchestras, the "Members only" clubs, people who flaunted their elitism through exclusivity, backgrounds that always assured that they were "in," and all others were "out," people who confused style with substance. Background was their armor. The great emphasis was always on tradition, the pattern of sameness, and privilege. He had always found these people vain, silly, haughty, and arrogant. Brought up materialistically, they were never satisfied, even though they had everything money could buy. They all drank too much, as he did, the liquor helping to keep feelings buried. The big alcoholic lie was that they were better than everyone else.

What he had always found most sickening about these people was their lack of innocence. That was why he hadn't married one of his own. He had chosen Kate. He had ignored his mother's protestations. He had never asked her what she thought about any of this. He had known his only chance was to make the decision without his mother, so he had eloped with Kate to the Bahamas. He had loved Kate very much. He had watched her make her debut as his wife, and she had always made an impact, which he liked. He had liked to show her off. And he desperately wanted her to have his child. Although she had never been forthright about her past, that hadn't mattered to Garrison. He loved her. Then she began pushing him out of her life, pushing him into other "friendships."

He continued to walk, ignoring the passersby, because in his mind, he saw only her. He had watched her struggle to become a well-known author. He had watched her exude sadness at painful reviews. He knew the insecurities. He also knew there was a place in his heart that only she could fill. . . .

Garrison put his key in the door. Kate was at the desk in the suite. Flowers were everywhere. She looked up from the desk so piled high with letters that the surface was lost to view.

"Do we have time to work on the baby?" he asked, coming over and kissing the side of her neck.

"I've got to talk to my agent, and Christine invited just the girls up for some champagne before the party. . . . I'm sorry."

He looked at her eyes, hard and uncaring about his desires.

"It seems we never have time anymore, Kate."

"Oh, God . . ." she began irritably, "you know how important tonight is to me. Do we have to talk about this now?"

"Why do you care so damn little about starting a family?"

"Why do you care so damn much? It's just not the right time, Garrison. I don't want to stop everything now and raise babies."

He looked at her. He felt like he was knocking against a sheet of iron in Kate's unmoving eyes. He was failing just as he always did in all their discussions on this topic.

"You don't want any children, period. Do you?"

"That's not true. Don't you believe me?"

Garrison could not remember what had caused the first small scratches of uneasiness, then the first stab of bewilderment, then the nagging pull of fear, as he began to doubt his wife's position. Maybe it was the "don't you believe me," which he had heard before, snapped in answer to his questions. Maybe it was the short replies she gave to all his inquiries. Maybe it was because he knew that honest people were never touchy about the matter of being trusted.

CHAPTER 18

*J*essie had gone for a late afternoon jog in Central Park. As a non–New Yorker, she was half curious and half fearful of running here, but it proved quite satisfying. Returning to the hotel, she showered and got out the new dress Sarah had helped her pick out earlier at Bergdorf's. The two of them and Christine had flown to New York for Kate's publishing party. Sarah had said she was having a drink with an old friend beforehand. Christine now came out of the bathroom, wrapped in a towel.

"Jessie, let's do our makeup together."

"You know I don't wear any."

"Be daring tonight," Christine laughed.

Over the next hour, the two girls talked of their children, the frustrations of the hotel, Jessie's new painting, and Lawton. They were embroiled in combat again, battling over his job, which was why he hadn't come to New York.

"Is it true?"

"What are you talking about?" Christine was instantly on guard, her blue eyes wary.

"Hey, Christine, this is me you're talking to."

The two women enjoyed each other's company. Over the years they had grown quite close. Jessie's first show at Seasons had blossomed into a career. That first connection had led to a warm friendship. And Christine owned a number of Jessica Malcolm pieces, which had doubled in value.

The tension in Christine's face eased. "I suppose Kate told you about Lawton?" Jessie nodded, not saying anything, waiting to see what Christine wanted to confide. "It's all true, every sordid, crazy bit of it. He's got this idea that he should, as he puts it, 'totally yield his hold on material things.' He wants to be the next Jimmy Swaggart or something. I'm telling you, Jessica, it's scary. Except for the times when it's almost funny. It's like a bad novel."

"How did it happen? I mean, what happened to him?"

Christine shrugged and the towel fell away from her soft naked shoulders. Jessica appreciated her friend's beauty with an artist's eye. How could any man be so stupid as to risk losing her?

"Midlife, maybe. Incipient insanity. Maybe I didn't give him something he needed."

Jessica laid a comforting hand on Christine's arm. "Stop it, Christine. Lawton is damaged. It's not your fault. Why doesn't he think about you and Alexandra?"

A moment of silence passed while Christine collected herself.

"How's Ned?" she asked, picking up her teal blue eye pencil.

"He's okay . . ." Jessie hesitated. "I just can't shake the guilt." Her eyes clouded. "I don't know if I can handle adultery any more, Christine. The pain is monumental. . . ."

"Let me see the dress you bought," Christine said, deliberately changing the subject in order to lift Jessie out of her sadness.

Jessie modeled her new outfit in front of the long dressing room mirror. She had picked out a black jersey Norma Kamali dress that clung to her attractively.

"It's beautiful," Christine approved. "My jewelry is in my bag next to the bed. Pick out something for tonight."

Jessie rummaged through the jewels that her friend had brought with her. "What are you wearing?"

"My black silk Valentino with the velvet jacket, and my sapphires." Christine went over to her bag. "Here, let me look." She sorted until she found a pair of emerald and diamond earrings with matching bracelet . . . a gift from Alfred.

"There," she pronounced. "Perfect."

Kate showed up a half hour later, entering the room glowing. She was wearing a blue and green beaded Valentino trimmed with black beaded piping—a real one—no copies for her anymore. She had had a makeup artist and hairdresser come to her room. She looked like a fashion model on the outside. Inside, she was quaking with nerves.

"I got a message from Sarah saying she was running late and she would meet us at the party," Kate said, and then the three of them spent an hour together in the suite, laughing, chatting, drinking champagne.

"We better get going," said Kate, looking at her watch nervously.

"One last toast to your great success with *Miracles*," Christine said.

Kate looked at her two friends and smiled. She had always distrusted the companionship of women . . . but she was happy to have them with her tonight. The three women hugged each other.

"Let's go . . . my publisher sent a limo for us."

———

Garrison had spent the afternoon walking distractedly around the perimeter of the park brooding over his wife, and now he sat on the floor, his head resting against the sofa in Sarah's hotel room. He was paying for her to have her own room, and he assumed she had made an appropriate explanation to the others.

He had begun to see Sarah secretly a few months ago. She was not really his type at all: She was like a jewel, cold and refined. In the beginning they played a lot of tennis . . . now occasionally they slept together.

"My mother left everything in my estate to my heir. A child I'll probably never have," he was saying. Suddenly, he saw his mother's burial—the open coffin, his mother's shrunken ravaged face twisted toward him with beseeching eyes. He rose to feet and wandered to the window.

"A child I'll probably never have," he repeated slowly, turning back to Sarah, who was slowly unfastening the buttons of her blouse. When she was fully naked, he took a long sip from his gin martini and watched her walk toward him.

The phone rang and no one picked it up as she touched him, then bent down to her knees, taking him in her mouth.

He strained his hips forward to meet her, grabbing her shoulders, burying himself in her warm, moist mouth. Then he made love to her with stiff, slow, precise desire.

Afterward, as he rolled over onto the carpet, he experienced an intense stab of pain and guilt: Kate.

The three girls wove their way through the crowd that was gathered near the entrance to the Rainbow Room. Photographers scrambled to get close to them. Kate was very aware of heads turning as she passed. Publishers, literary agents, editors, and the press chatted in groups. The publishing world was small, and everyone knew each other.

"Go help yourself to some champagne, girls," she waved them on as a photographer sidetracked her. She could hardly contain the excitement that coursed through her. Not for a second did she wonder—or care—where her husband was.

Kate signed copies of *Miracles* for some of the guests, then posed for photos with her editor.

After a while, Kate excused herself to go to the rest room. As she was about to reapply lipstick, she looked in the mirror and froze at the sight of the woman who just entered.

"You stole my book!" Lisa hissed, brandishing a copy of *Miracles*. "After all the help I gave you. I launched your career, for goodness sake. How could you? First you talk the publisher out of putting my name on the jacket of the hotel scandal book and now this! I would have helped you, Kate. That's the thing I don't understand. Why didn't you ask?"

It was true that Kate had used Lisa mercilessly, imposing on her to help with the second book even though she'd backed out on her promise to share the credit for the first one. Kate consoled herself that at least she had given Lisa her share of the advance money, so she didn't really renege. It's just that Lisa never got an author's credit.

Kate had stayed with Lisa to finish up the celebrity biography. At the same time, Kate was also struggling with her novel. No matter what she did, it wouldn't come out right; the words wouldn't flow. One night Lisa had been at a concert and Kate had found the manuscript in her closet. She had taken it to an all-night copy shop. It was like some demon whispered the plan in her ear, dictated every move. By the time Lisa returned, the copy was safely tucked away in Kate's suitcase, and Lisa was none the wiser.

"Then why didn't you give it to Eric to sell? I just wanted to know how you put it together. I didn't think about anything else. But when time went by . . ." Kate stopped in midsentence. Lisa was looking right through her, and her eyes screamed in Kate's face that she was a liar—a liar and a fraud. Kate tried another tactic.

"Lisa, be honest. You couldn't have made the success out of this book that I did. Look at the crowd. Do you think they would have bought a book with your name on it?" As she spoke, Kate warmed up to her own story. "Do you think they would come to see you? My name put this book over the top, and you know it!"

The words were cruel and there was an element of truth to them, just enough to make Kate swallow her own lie. But Lisa only became angrier. Even if Kate's name could sell copies, she couldn't get away with plagiarism. It was a crime.

"Don't you realize what you've done? What I could do to you?"

Kate's face went white.

"I have every intention of going to your publisher with

this, Kate. I'm going to destroy you. This is *my* book, *my* best-seller!"

"You can't do that," Kate breathed. "And you won't," she went on, stronger. She had known this day might come and was not unprepared. "You remember your little secret from college, don't you?"

"What?"

Kate's smile was the look of not having outthought, but having outsmarted someone. "You know exactly what I'm talking about, Lisa, so don't you dare try to threaten me."

Lisa saw the crumpled boy lying on the road, his eyes staring at nothing. She had made the mistake of sharing her most intimate secret with Kate Robinson years ago.

"We should go back before we're missed," Kate said. She reached for Lisa's arm, but the other woman wrestled free.

Lisa wasn't going anywhere near Kate Robinson's publication party. And not only because the book being celebrated was rightfully hers. The other reason had been brought about by an ingrained habit of hers—one that came from her gifts as an author. Lisa possessed the writer's insatiable need to know and dig into everyone around her, even strangers. She was an inveterate eavesdropper and reader of other people's papers. She had wanted to know who else was in Kate's circle, who else might be at the party, so when the publisher's publicist stepped away from her position at the door to the Rainbow Room, Lisa took the opportunity to snoop. She didn't doubt for a minute that Sarah Potter was the same Sarah Potter with whom she shared a terrible secret. She knew Sarah had moved to Palm Beach. More than that, she could guess what kind of friends Sarah would make there. Kate and Sarah were a perfect match.

Suddenly another woman came into the bathroom and

Kate reapplied her public smile. She was afraid to let Lisa loose among her guests, but she had no choice. Where was Garrison? she finally asked herself as she went back to the party.

Finally, she spotted him. She sighed with relief.

"Where have you been?"

"I went for a walk . . . lost track of time. I'm sorry."

"Please stay by my side. It would mean a great deal to me tonight," she whispered.

Garrison read into her voice a need he did not often hear. "You've written a great book, Kate. Don't worry," he added.

"Please just don't leave me," she pleaded, lifting his hand up to her lips for a quick kiss. Her limbs trembled. The unmistakable aroma of another woman's most private scent was on his fingers.

Kate felt sick. But she knew she had no one to blame but herself. She had driven him to it—and for the sake of her career, she knew she would continue to push him into another woman's arms.

"What's wrong, Katie?"

"Nothing, I'm fine." And of all the lies she had ever told in her life, that was one of the biggest.

Garrison had stayed by his wife's side the remainder of the evening. He now sat alone in the living room of their suite. He took a long sip from his gin martini. The walls seemed to swallow him. In the beginning, he felt fated to get ensnared in the spider's web of emotions that made up the relationship between him, Kate, and Sarah. But tonight, it was the knowledge that neither his marriage nor his affair had any meaning whatever that was destroying him.

When he entered the bedroom, he still wore his dress clothes and his wife was still awake, despite the late hour.

He gazed at her wearily.

"I think the party was very successful," she began. "There was a good turnout."

He stood wishing he had not come in here at all. Wasn't it foolish of him to expect to win the affection of one so attached to her career?

"What a waste we've become, Kate." His eyes probed hers for an answer. "What a waste," he repeated slowly, his words weighted with drops of gin.

"Come to bed, Garrison, and let's make love," he heard her say softly. "We can't have a baby without that."

CHAPTER 19

$\mathcal{M}$aria put down her book. The mild drizzle of earlier in the evening had become a downpour. She got out of bed and stood at the window, looking out at the storm, wondering if it were raining in New York, for Kate's book signing. Hundreds of miles away, she could feel the festivities. She could envision the crowd, the people mingling together, looking at each other, waiting for the place or the party to give them meaning. She felt the four friends with their laughter and gentle intimacies. She knew it was not really as it seemed.

Maria knew human beings do this a lot to each other.

They do not seek to lift their friends; they seek to play games, or use them. They do not truly listen to each other or become fully involved; they are moved to go for something for themselves. Some of these girls were blinder and more helpless than any animal. An animal knows who its friends are and who are its enemies. Animals know when to defend themselves. They do not expect a friend to come in and slit their throat.

Maria felt pain. She knew she could not tell these girls how to live their lives, what to do, and what not to do. She knew the only grace they could have was the grace they could see for themselves. If they couldn't picture it . . . they would never have peace.

A fear went through Maria in a spasm. She looked out at the dark sky, knowing she must get some sleep. Lately, she had been terribly overworked, and tomorrow would be another busy day with Detective Gus. So she forced herself to think of Michael, the little lost boy she had helped locate yesterday in the Everglades. His presence left her with a patina of calm. Maria fell into a heavy sleep that was at once invaded by a dream. . . .

She awoke with a start just before dawn, with pounding heart and an icy chill. She could see the King of Spades . . . she could see the face of someone hurtling headlong toward death. She could see a wound to the back of the head that came before the drowning water. She could see a female face from a great distance; it was straining and failing to come closer. She could hear angry words. She struggled to make her dream clearer, but the words fled from her memory, and she was left with only a fading apparition.

She got up out of bed, understanding with fierce clarity that one of her friends was doomed.

Gus was standing outside Maria's front door. There were rings of sweat under his arms and it wasn't even eight yet.

"Good morning, Gus. I've made us some coffee," Maria said after opening the door.

"In this envelope is twenty thousand dollars," Gus said as he sat down at the kitchen table. "It was found on the floor at the airport in Key West. It was part of the ransom money for little Michael and must have been dropped in the rush."

"What else do you have?"

"Not much. The husband withdrew the two hundred thousand from his savings and left it in the locker as instructed. No word if the wife is still alive."

Maria, still in her robe, looked both worried and puzzled. Her gray hair was pulled back from her patrician-looking face, marred by deep wrinkles. She stared at the envelope, but didn't pick it up. Threatening at the margin of her consciousness was the shadow of her dream. She knew she wouldn't be able to tune into anything so long as the other issue was trespassing in her mind.

"Gus, do you mind just leaving it with me . . . now is not the time for this, I'm afraid."

"Yes, of course. When would you like me to come back?" he asked.

"I'll call you."

"Fine." He hesitated. "You all right?"

"I'll be fine."

CHAPTER 20

*J*essie sat in the restaurant, waiting for Maria, with whom she was having lunch. Her mind drifted, as it often did, to the beginning of her love affair with Ned. She was always on tenterhooks around him, always afraid that she was saying or doing the wrong thing. He never uttered a word of reproach for her awkwardness. He was patient and generous about her mistakes, those terrible moments when a burst of blood to her cheekbones told her that she had said or done the wrong thing. He never showed any displeasure with her, though. Two, three, four times a week, he would drive up to the back door of the gallery at the closing hour and take her for long rides along the ocean. Or they would go to her house, she would cook dinner, and then he would insist she paint. And he got along really well with Allison, often insisting she accompany them if she were at the gallery after school.

He was habitually restless. She never knew where he was, in what city or on what continent. Their meetings always happened unexpectedly, with a kind of peculiar abruptness, as if he had not intended to see her, but something burst within him. She liked that, because he was a continuous presence in her life, like a ray of the sun, that could hit her at any given moment.

There were moments when she felt sudden, violent longings for him, though she was not unhappy during his absences. Jessica knew a relationship needed both intimacy and distance. She used the time away from him to make progress in her own career. She worked full-time now as the manager of the gallery on Worth Avenue, and continued her own painting.

She understood little of him. Intimacy made him nervous. He was reluctant to smile too much, as if giving something away. His cupboard of life, emotionally speaking, was nearly bare, yet she cared for him. Occasionally, she would find enormous spreads of flowers standing in her living room. He offered her money once, so she could stay home to paint instead of work, and she refused it with such a painful flare of anger that he apologized immediately.

She had never wondered if Ned was good-looking or not; when he entered a room, it was impossible to look at anyone else. His power and appeal came not from his looks or his money, but from what he made people feel about themselves. Jessie's emotions sped to the surface in his presence.

Things became what they were for the moment. She abandoned herself to him, to anything he wished. She was sure he had taught her every manner of sensuality that existed. His passionate carnality had unlocked eroticism that she never dreamed she possessed. The shame from her childhood had always tainted her during her marriage, but Ned had helped erase all that.

Ned never spoke of his wife, but Sarah once had explained to Jessie that his marriage was merely a necessary convenience, for the sake of the vast fortune. Jessie forced herself not to talk or think about it; she didn't understand it, and as a result, in her heart, she felt shame. Shame for being with a married man. Yet he was the man she wanted.

She then spotted Maria entering the restaurant, moving with her typical gliding, graceful step, like that of a stately swan floating on calm water. Jessie rose from her seat and embraced her. In Maria's presence, she always felt an inexplicable sensation of absolute calm. She was unable to account for the impact Maria had on her, yet she was grateful for the respite it gave her from her concerns. Maria was the only friend with whom she could discuss anything. Jessie looked at Maria's face. It bore no mark of pain, fear, or guilt, only serene determination and certainty. And incredible intelligence.

Jessie had warmed to Maria from their very first meeting years ago, from the very first touch of her hand. Maria saw the world as a place eagerly worth knowing, and that was how Jessie wanted to feel.

"Hello, my friend."

"Hello, Maria."

"I have a book for Allison. Don't let me forget to give it to you before we leave. It's a book on angels. . . . I think she'll enjoy it."

The two ordered iced tea, and then Maria asked a few questions and Jessie began to talk about her relationship with her ex-husband, Ned, and Allison, and, of course, her girl-friends. Christine had been very good to her from the begin-ning and always hung her paintings in her hotel; Kate, whom Jessie didn't care for all that much, but Christine loved her, so that was good enough for her; and Sarah, Allison's tennis teacher, whom Jessie saw regularly. They were all very dif-ferent, but it worked.

"I still cannot believe how relationships fall apart," she was saying with reference to a couple she knew who had been married twenty-five years and were suddenly divorc-ing.

"No relationship falls apart unless there is one more im-portant waiting for you," Maria told her. "Did you read the books I gave you?"

"Knowledge is not bringing me a clearer vision, Maria. It's only making the mystery greater."

"Answers and explanations, if you desire them, shall be given you in due time. Have patience . . . and don't be afraid to keep searching."

"Life used to be so simple. Before I knew anything," Jessie said, smiling.

"Change is inevitable. It is even something to be cherished . . . however, at the moment of transition, it is not comforting or easy."

"How do I know if I'm on the right path?" she asked, picking at her chicken salad.

"True spiritual progress is shown in the cheerful, sincere life of the person possessing it, and in the encouraging and ennobling influence that person's life has on others," replied Maria, the earnestness of her voice like a hand extended in support. "You do that, Jessie . . . for many people."

"Why am I with Ned? A married man? That can't be spiritual progress!" she exclaimed with exasperation.

"That which guides two people together and binds them in love, Jessie, is a mystery. There are no rational explanations."

As if controlled by a magnet, Jessie's thoughts went back to Ned. Passion had been sustaining their relationship, but she knew a lasting foundation would have to be built from something else.

"Tell me, how is Christine?" Maria asked, as if sensing the need to take Jessie's mind off her own troubles.

"Busy, very busy." Jessie then hesitated. "Do you think they're happily married? They always look so happy."

Maria's eyes became faraway, as if she were gazing at a point yards behind Jessie's head. She knew there was no fulfillment, but an emptying of personality, resulting from two needy individuals who use each other, but never really meet as two human beings.

"Nothing is at it appears to be, Jessie," she said, "even when one is certain. There's nothing as deceptive as one's outward appearance, the facade. Almost everyone disguises their true self."

"Well, she and Lawton seem happier than Kate and Garrison. Kate is never around."

"Kate has no concept of how much time and effort it takes to make a relationship work."

"I don't think anyone, married or not, has the key to what makes a relationship work. I don't think Sarah is that ecstatic with her situation."

"Sarah doesn't demand as much of life as you do," Maria told her.

"She's lucky," Jessie commented as her mind prowled in

evasive circles around the core Sarah and she had in common: guilt.

While Jessica loved Ned and would forever thank him for giving her back her sensuality, still, her guilt over their relationship drove her as a locomotive pulls a train. She sensed the same core in Sarah though the other woman never expressed it. Jessica had painted a quick portrait of Sarah on a paper napkin while they were dawdling over lunch. The sketch captured an aura around Sarah that Jessica could totally relate to since it mirrored her own. Jessica never saw Sarah in the same light after that. Maria, too, had seen this in Sarah and had mentioned it in passing in the group readings. But while Jessica's guilt was obvious, Sarah hid hers behind a wall of drugs and denial and its source remained her secret.

She and Maria talked effortlessly for a few hours before Jessie had to go home to Allison.

"You promise we'll do this again soon?" Jessie said, hugging her friend.

"I promise," Maria said affectionately, sensing Jessie clutching at her presence as if it were something life-giving.

CHAPTER 21

$\mathcal{J}$essie heard the papery slap of cards flung down in jubilation.

"Hi, I'm home."

"I won," Allison cried with a golden laugh. "We're playing war."

"How was your tennis lesson?" Jessie asked, affectionately fingering the strands of her daughter's hair.

"Great."

"I thought I was going to die of the heat today," Sarah said, "but it didn't seem to bother your daughter. She's going to be one terrific tennis player, by the way."

Allison blushed like a tomato. "Sarah's going to babysit me tonight, Mom, 'cause you have a date."

Jessie looked at her daughter. It was the attitude of the head, the awareness—perceiving, receiving. And the eyes saw everything; above, behind, and through. The little girl who always dressed like a boy, rejecting dresses altogether. The one who put all her dolls under the bed. Allison had grown into such an independent spirit, with such strong opinions. She had a vibrant personality, a great imagination, and a wonderful sense of humor.

Jessie smiled inwardly. She had promised herself that she would raise a child who knew how to please herself, not her. When Jessie was growing up, she had a curly-haired wish for long, straight hair. She had the wish for no freckles. She tried to please her mother. Now she wanted her daughter to be the only authority on how she wanted to look. She wanted her to be able to walk past the mirror without consulting it . . . she wanted her to please herself . . . to turn her own face to the world.

"Do you have homework?"

"Yep."

"What?"

"I have to write a story using all my spelling words."

"Well, get going . . . tonight I'm sure you'll find better things to do," she winked at Sarah.

Allison lightly ran her fingertips over her lips and then her mother's, before hopping up and going over to Sarah.

"See you tonight, Sarah Bearah," she said, pecking her lightly on the cheek.

"Thanks for picking her up from school," said Jessie, looking at her friend.

"Any time, you know that."

Sarah was so good to her daughter. Last year when Allison had a biking accident, Sarah came every day to the hospital to relieve Jessie so she could work. Every time she needed a babysitter at the last moment, Sarah was there. And no matter what she did in the privacy of her rented room, Sarah was rigorous about staying straight around Allison. In fact, Allison probably knew a side of Sarah that no one else ever saw.

Although Jessica and Sarah were so opposite, they had grown to love each other with a generosity in their friendship that was rare. Their friendship was an offshoot of the foursome because, unlike Kate and Christine, they were still searching, or anyway, still single.

"How's Alfred?" asked Jessica.

"He's great, but he's in Hong Kong."

"And Garrison?"

"I haven't seen him much."

Jessica couldn't condemn Sarah for her affair with Garrison. She had no right to condemn anyone. Betrayal, deceit, cheating—she was guilty of them all. She just wished she and Sarah could talk more openly about the guilt they had in common. They both slept with married men . . . but Sarah didn't seem to suffer like she did. She remained hidden behind her protective wall. Jessica slumped in her chair, thinking of the honesty she could no longer claim. Ned had told her in the beginning that it was her proud purity he loved. And now her love for him was threatening to destroy it. Guilt and shame. Jessica wanted in that moment to ask Sarah if she ever felt those things, but she knew her friend would take offense if she dared. Sarah was very secretive.

"I heard Ned shunted his wife off to Europe again."

"Yeah, we're having dinner. That's why I need you tonight."

"Well, what time?"

"Eight?"

"I'll be here."

"After Sarah left, Jessie went into her studio. Pots of gardenias were scattered everywhere, their fragile petals like fresh cream against their dark leaves. There was a large portrait of Allison that glowed over the room.

Jessie luxuriated in the solitude. She had missed privacy when she was married.

An empty canvas was perched on the easel. The sight of it made her smile. Working allowed her to keep her body and soul together. When she painted, she could put behind her the madness of the past. It was the only time her memory-bound mind permitted that.

She put on her favorite Beatles song, "Blackbird," picked up her brush, and a lovely flush enveloped her face with the very first stroke. A calm and peaceful serenity descended sweetly over her.

When Ned's wife came into his study, she was dressed for traveling. In her hand was her itinerary and a list of the things she wanted attended to in her absence.

Ned was on the phone to one of his various offices. He was discussing the rumored merger of an airline and an oil company. His desk was strewn with the morning papers. He had been working for hours. His study had a spiral staircase that led up to a private bath, shower, and dressing room. He had slept in the study last night.

"Just a minute," he mouthed, his hand over the receiver.

"I'll phone you later . . ." she said, and kissed the air near his cheek, then walked out.

He stared after her. Introspection was not a thing Ned ever had time for. For some reason, this morning he did.

After he hung up, Ned pictured Jessie in his mind. He wondered how much his wife knew about his affair with Jessie—and how much she cared. He pictured her laughing . . . making fun of his midlife fling.

As if that was all it was. . . .

In his mind, there was an ever-present image of Jessie when they first met, with her direct green eyes that had disturbed him and made him want to discard all that was inconsequential out of the path between them. In the beginning he had wanted only to slake his thirst for her, or so he thought. That was where it started.

But early in their affair it became clear to him that all that had been tangential in his life before he met Jessie was now at center stage. The years of pushing away everything but money and the things it provided began to fade. Everything he valued flip flopped and his need for her kept growing. Until now, a day away from Jessie was torture. He was beginning to realize that his work and his money were ways to spend time until he could see Jessie, and that she was the life force and everything else was just filler. His passion for her had taken him over.

In the beginning, they had seen each other only occasionally. He had not gone to see her the day after they first made love. Indeed, he had awakened in the morning hating himself for telling her he would see her again. But need drew him back, need stronger than will, and before he knew it he was thinking of being with her all the time.

But in the beginning, though he had been flabbergasted

by Jessie's passion, he had never entertained the idea of divorcing his wife. It had never occurred to him he couldn't have both.

But time changed them all. Now she was not only desirable, she was impressive. How funny to think that at first he thought she was purity personified. He had learned that Jessie was not only pure but also passionate. She was always complex, never the same, and the more mature she became, the more he desired her. The artist in her fed the woman, and the more successful her art, the more perfect she was as a woman. How he wanted her. And how it killed him to know that she couldn't be completely his—not until he divorced his wife. And then who would he be and would Jessie still want him? Lately it seemed most of his days were spent tortured by thoughts like these. It almost made him resent her.

Was this love? He had no idea. Before Ned had turned twenty, he was already wearing masks. In due course, some of the masks became second nature. Not even Ned knew anymore where artifice began or ended.

He walked back to his desk, trying to keep Jessie out of focus. He sat looking down ... immersing her in a fog, struggling not to let her take any form. Only that which exists possesses identity, he told himself.

He forced himself to pick up the phone and call his stockbroker. He ordered him to purchase some shares from a company he had an inside tip on. He knew he would make a lot of money; however, that thought brought him nothing but boredom. What do you want? the enemy voice asked. His thoughts slipped again down that dangerous blind alley. She had become too important. Jessie was interfering with his life.

CHAPTER 22

They sat at a table for two on the back deck of his yacht, facing the darkness. Here they had their privacy. It had been their rendezvous spot for years. They were having an after-dinner glass of champagne. Jessie was barely aware of the boat; the only thing that held her attention was the full moon. It brought her a sense of inner peace, a serenity that amazed her.

"That will be all for tonight, Edward . . . thank you," Ned said to his butler.

"What are you thinking?" Jessie asked when Ned began to stare at her, not speaking. His eyes, which to her always seemed to reflect the light, hiding his expressions, looked for a moment as if the masks were gone.

"A penny for your thoughts," she went on.

"I . . ." he began, then stopped.

Ned stood up and took her by the hand, holding her close. He did not know why her presence made him want to confess things. She lifted him from a plane even he could not define. Ned led her to the master stateroom. Without a word he took off her clothes until she was naked before him.

He stood across the room looking at her. She was desirable beyond utterance. With her, every time was just like the first time they had made love.

He walked toward her. He reached and moved a lock of her hair from her cheek, cautiously, as if it were fragile. He held her hair back with his fingertips and pressed his mouth to hers. The kiss was tender, but the way his fingers held her hair was more urgent, almost a grip of despair. She emitted a natural aroma that held him instantaneously captive. Then he touched her . . . and fire ignited and blazed.

The bedroom had the scent of sex . . . it permeated everything. Jessie lay very still, on the verge of sleep, savoring the warm, lingering pleasure between her legs. Ned held her silently in his arms, and she lay there comforted, her hips jutting softly into his groin.

"I want you again," he whispered, as his fingers gently traced oval patterns on her back.

"I need to sleep . . ." she replied, reaching behind her, patting his leg.

Inside he was seething with frustrated excitement again. He had to have her. With his fingers, he began to stroke the

nook of her buttocks, then down farther to the region between her thighs. He pressed his hardness against her back
with a passion he had never felt before. He wanted to punish
her for making him feel all these strong emotions.

"I want you now."

"No, Ned . . . not now. I have to leave soon."

He heard nothing. He held her body and entered her so
abruptly and with such force, it hurt her. He pushed and
pushed into her as if the violence of the way he took her
could wipe his emotions for her out of existence. She felt a
pain rip through her.

The shock became a numbness spreading through her
body. She felt tight pressure in her stomach. She was conscious of convulsion. Bile clogged her throat.

"Never force me, Ned!" she screamed. "Never. Do you
hear me? *Never!*"

Jessie got out of bed. She stood in the suffocating darkness
trembling with hatred, fright, disgust. This entry from the
rear . . . without her permission . . . it was a violation. She
had so carefully distanced herself from that act . . . an act that
took place without her permission long ago. She remembered when no cry or protest availed her. She remembered
the hand that slithered up between her thighs under her
nightgown. The hand, with its rigid middle finger, working
with haste, probing inside her, causing her pain. Now, standing here, she felt the same pain again. She was filled with
revulsion. Once again, her soul had been looted.

CHAPTER 23

Sarah sat listening to Chopin. The music opened the doors of her mind, allowing her to forget everything and just feel.

She took a sip of her champagne. Her fourth glass. Today was the anniversary of her father's death . . . ironically also, the very day she found out she was pregnant.

She wondered how long she would be able to teach and work at the tennis shop. Pregnant tennis instructors weren't exactly in demand, she smiled ruefully to herself and took a large gulp of champagne. She really must stop drinking immediately. Sarah held the champagne glass up to the light.

She tried to imagine the look on her mother's face when she found out Sarah was pregnant, "in the family way," "preggers," however her prim and proper uptight mother might refer to it. How about knocked up? Sarah laughed and poured more champagne into her glass. Her mother . . . that pillar of control and propriety. Her mother who had always been cruel in her moral demands on her. Hopefully her mother would have a heart attack and die and then Sarah could support her baby.

They hadn't spoken even once since Sarah had left Poughkeepsie that fateful night nearly thirteen years ago. She received dictums through the accountant and had managed to keep her trust fund, but that was all. And the truth was, she didn't want to rely on it anymore. What she wanted more than anything was for the father of her baby to take care of her so she wouldn't have to take her mother's money. Her behavior was shameful enough to her. For her mother, it was a weapon to be used against her.

Whose baby was it? In her loneliness in Palm Beach, she tried to fill the hole in her heart, as usual, with physical pleasures . . . drugs, alcohol, sex. There was Alfred. . . . They had been seated next to each other on New Year's Eve a year ago, at the Everglades Club. Until that time, she had never been able to get near to him, but his wife had died, and he had begun dating. What she saw in the florid face that night was the unmistakable look of power, and she was drawn to it. They had both been more than a little drunk, left their respective dates on the dance floor at two A.M., and took off together . . . not to return for a week. They went straight to the airport, boarded Alfred's plane, and headed to Milan. Upon landing, a car and driver were waiting to take them to Lake Como. They stayed at the Hotel Villa d'Este for three days. The weather had been glorious, the sun burned on the mountains, and the lake was like lapis lazuli. They played golf, took long walks, boat rides—and had lots of sex.

When they returned to Florida, she boldly embarked on a plot to get him. He had that power of certainty that she was attracted to. He also exuded energy and danger. She sent him streams of letters expressing obsessive adoration. Rumor was her mother thought she was dating a gangster.

She knew he was the talk of the town because of his money. She knew his name was only known in business circles, not social circles. She knew he was an outsider from New York, immensely secretive, and of course had been blackballed from *all* the clubs. He was known for his addictions to women and drinking, yet he never stopped talking about the things he was going to do for *her*...he was extremely generous. He was also honest with her. He told her he had no intention of remarrying and was doggedly evasive about the other women in his life.

So Sarah had stopped taking the pill. She had let her imagination go...telling herself Alfred would take care of her; he would have to if she got pregnant.

Her fingers rested limply around the stem of the glass. She reflected with pain on some of her lonesome drinking bouts, and her one-night stands. She was tired of being alone... tired of trying to make ends meet. She wanted to count on someone again. Alfred did listen to her, and he did give her an inward assurance that filled her with joy. He brought her ease and security. She had a certain dependence on him, and she could ask him advice of any kind. He would lecture her with the same ponderous intensity her father had. She actually had become rather attached to him...and his money.

And what if Garrison were the father? How would she ever be able to face her three friends again? They were all she had. The thought of facing Kate was the least difficult. She worried more what Christine would think. And Allison, who was old enough to understand what it meant to have a baby with somebody else's daddy.

Well, that was the point. Garrison wasn't anyone's daddy and that was Kate's fault.

The wind chimes outside Sarah's room startled her out of her morose reverie. She should just assume it was Alfred's baby. It was logical; he was safe, and she wouldn't have to totally destroy anyone's marriage that way.

Sarah went to the date book she kept assiduously and counted back over the month to see if she could determine who she had been with during her peak fertility days. The nineteenth: dinner at the Bath and Tennis Club. Sarah chewed the pencil as she tried to remember who she was with, but she drew a blank. It could easily have been one of the times Kate asked her to accompany Garrison. Or it might have been that she and Alfred went separately and ended up in bed together afterward. Or she might have gone with Garrison and met up with Alfred later. The twentieth: dinner with Alfred at Cafe L'Europe—that was pretty straightforward. Unless she had been with Garrison during the day. Twenty-second: cocktail party at the Watleys. Anything was possible because she probably partied long afterward into the night. It was pointless to try and figure it out this way, leastways when she was drunk.

Garrison was sweet though he seemed to fade in and out over the span of an evening. His love-making was different than Alfred's, less powerful, more demanding in a different way. Garrison needed her, but not in a repulsive way. Oddly enough, it was his need that drew her to him, made her feel like she had something to give someone. He was probably the only person in the whole world who ever relied on her for anything, even if it were only sex. Garrison was caring. Kate would be crazy to just throw him away. But Sarah was in no position to catch him if she did.

What was the use? She might as well just get rid of it. The spoon next to her bed beckoned and Sarah dipped it in the white powder trying to recall the article she had read about when a fetus was most vulnerable to cocaine addiction. As she held the white powder to her nostril a picture flashed through her head. Her baby. For the first time in Sarah's life she thought about somebody else. She put the spoon down, went to the bathroom, and poured her best bath bubbles into the tub.

———

Someone was banging on the door. As Sarah stood up she felt a heaviness that was different than her old familiar friend, the hangover. As woozy as she felt, it was pleasant to know it was a natural reaction instead of chemicals poisoning her system.

Kate barged in before Sarah could completely struggle out of bed.

"Hi. You're sleeping late." Sarah nodded weakly. "You look terrible. Are you sick?"

"I love you too!" How long before she told her friends, Sarah wondered. She should figure out what she was going to do about it first. "You're back a day early, aren't you?"

"The Seychelles were nice, but too quiet. Garrison was boring beyond belief. I had to get out of there. All he wants is to work on having a baby. It's tiresome, really."

Kate turned toward the mirror hanging over Sarah's bureau. Sarah kept hats on the pegs surrounding the large glass and now Kate took an oversized straw sunbonnet from its peg and mugged for the mirror.

"I need a favor," she said. "I've got to go to New York to do some research. But I promised Garrison I'd go to the Bath and Tennis dance Friday night. . . . Will you fill in for me?"

Sarah hesitated. "Please, Sarah. I don't want to leave him on the loose. I'm not that stupid."

Something inside Sarah cracked open. These women friends were so dear to her, each in her own way. Sometimes she felt like a pitiful creature they had taken in when she most needed them, and she didn't want to lose them. Suddenly holding on to Garrison seemed so less important than holding on to Kate.

"Come on, I'll make you some coffee," Kate offered. "Will you do it?" she called from the kitchenette. "Please."

"Okay." Sarah hoped she could babysit for Garrison and not sleep with him.

"You're a love," Kate said. The smell of the coffee made Sarah nauseous—and she ran to the bathroom before Kate could ask any questions. When she emerged, she saw the note Kate had left behind: "Got to run. Don't drink so much. Then you won't be having 'morning sickness.' Hah hah—Love, K. And thanks."

If only Kate hadn't pushed them together, one side of her argued, but in her heart, Sarah knew that she had violated her friend's trust. The shield she had hidden behind all these years was beginning to crumble and she felt awful.

CHAPTER 24

"*L*et me explain something to you, asshole." There was no politeness in Alfred Blum's voice. "Don't strong-arm me —what I know about you could send you to prison." He blew out cigar smoke and narrowed his eyes. He threw the latest issue of *Esquire* onto the floor. An article had described him as a man of ample proportions. He was furious.

Behind his back, Alfred Blum was accused of being a mean son-of-a-bitch. People feared his wrath. Alfred looked upon his unpopularity in the business world as mere jealousy. He had inherited his family's desire to amass great wealth, and he was good at it. He also loved to talk about it. His only other passion was sex.

He put his cigar in his mouth and puffed on it. He thought about all of the important men that disliked him or that he had done battle with. He certainly hoped an unauthorized biography did not loom ahead. Alfred was a keeper of secrets; he couldn't confide, and he wanted no one prying. He made it a point to be very polite to Kate Robinson these days. Thankfully, she seemed to be writing only trashy novels, but she was one broad who could really do him damage if she put her mind to it. He squirmed at the idea of revealing anything, either by choice or accident. Whenever the press asked him for an interview, as they had a few minutes ago, he turned them down. He knew that any man who is doing all the talking isn't learning.

Alfred glanced down at the tote bag next to his desk. Inside was a Fabergé egg he had just bought for Sarah at an estate sale.

His wife had died of liver failure two years ago. Her true suicide was slow; she had embalmed herself with alcohol. Alfred knew he was an alcoholic, too, and attracted to another one . . . Sarah.

In the beginning, it had been a game, wanting to date all kinds of girls, staying out late, partying. He surrounded himself with beauty and youth. He liked dating the little girls from Palm Beach; these girls who never spoke directly to a waiter in their life. He would take these privileged females and make them maids to him. But Sarah had been different, free of the horrendous conventions that afflicted the hypocritical culture of Palm Beach. She sent him sexy love letters and tried to get him to diet and exercise to deal with his weight. She was even helping him with his tennis game, which he hadn't practiced in years. Unlike so many of the Palm Beach snobs, Sarah looked up to him, always asking his advice. She had such a childlike desire to be loved. He appreciated her helplessness. Small things like balancing her checkbook, paying bills, little everyday things confounded her.

There were still other women in his life, but at the moment, now that he and Christine no longer got together, Sarah was definitely his favorite. With her, he could have an orgasm and then be ready again a half hour later, as it had been with Christine.

Often he thought he would have been the happiest man on earth if he hadn't lost his son. He had so wanted to build a dynasty, but that wish was lost to him when his only son had been taken away in an instant. He had kept the story of his son's death hushed up. The accident had been listed as a hit-and-run, period. No one would ever know that the autopsy revealed heroin in his son's bloodstream. He still mourned privately for his child, but had forced himself painfully through that abysmal darkness. Still, he had learned that there were some things in life that even the passing of time couldn't obliterate.

Alfred Blum's dinner parties were always an experience. The food was prepared by his own French chef, and the wine was always superb, from his own well-stocked cellar.

The convivial sounds of voices talking and laughing could be heard from the living room. Waiters circulated unobtrusively with trays of Taittinger rosé.

Sarah waved at the two security guards, armed with pistols and dressed in identical navy blue blazers. She was late. She had been primping, trying to find just the right dress for tonight. Tonight she would break the news to Alfred.

"Where have you been?" Christine asked, kissing Sarah on both cheeks.

"It's been one of those days. Where's Lawton?"

"He's conducting a Bible study group tonight," Christine told her.

Sarah didn't comment. Everyone in town knew there was trouble in their marriage. And Sarah didn't understand how Christine put up with all that religious bullshit of his.

The two gossiped a little about who was there.

"You look marvelous, darling," said an old friend of Sarah's mother. She was small and birdlike, with Cupid's bow lips. Sarah was surprised to see her here, then she remembered, she had recently had to sell her mansion on the ocean. *Now* Alfred's parties were good enough for her.

Then she saw Alfred. His massiveness filled the room. He looked older than he was and although not handsome, there was something compelling and irresistible about him. His aura of power was his great aphrodisiac.

"I thought you forgot me," he whispered, kissing her on the lips.

The guests were seated at one long table in the main dining room that was decorated with six immense Venetian sterling silver candelabra. Beside each guest's plate was a gift, wrapped in gold and white paper: Cartier lighters for the men, gold swizzle sticks for the ladies. The candlelight was shining on the polished mahogany, the paintings, and the fine silver, as a sumptuous meal was served.

Sarah stared down at her seafood Newburg for thirty seconds before tasting it. She felt nauseous. She didn't know if it was her pregnancy or an incipient hangover.

More champagne was poured.

Alfred was tapping his fork against the side of his glass

and toasting his Japanese friends, for whom he was having this dinner.

More wine was served. She was getting slightly tipsy. She could see Alfred through the white anthurium of the centerpiece. She excused herself to go to the bathroom.

———

Alfred watched Sarah walk away. Her eggshell satin dress shimmered like heavy cream. He pretended to be listening to the woman next to him, but he was thinking only of Sarah.

She had brought him a newborn contentment, guaranteed sexual fulfillment. He could scarcely contain his passion for her. He ached with desire for her at that very moment.

———

Sarah sat back down. Oh, how she wished she had a line; however, lately, when she had her bouts with cocaine, the next day her home always seemed rimmed by four empty walls, extreme silence, and paranoia. And now . . . there was the baby to think about.

They were being served raspberries and red currants over homemade ice cream for dessert, Alfred's favorite. Sarah had more champagne. She was trying to carry on a conversation with the man next to her, but her words were blurring a little from the alcohol. She thought this meal would never end.

Coffee for the ladies was served in the living room, while the men went into the library for after-dinner port. The room was still cloudy with blue cigar smoke from before dinner. Sarah loathed cigars, but she had never dared say anything to Alfred.

She had another glass of champagne. Suddenly, she began to feel woozy . . . and then she remembered she had hidden some cocaine in the guest house. One little line couldn't hurt. She needed to sober up so she could tell Alfred her news later.

An hour passed and Alfred was getting tired of entertaining the Japanese moguls who were here looking for companies to buy. He respected their business acumen, but the truth was, the Japanese were not great assets at a social event. He allowed the conversation to wind down, hoping his guests would begin to go so that he could be alone with Sarah.

Sarah was really high. The ladies in the living room added their own cigarette smoke to the layer of blue cigar stench and Sarah knew she would not be able to stay inside without disgracing herself. Her watch said twelve-thirty. She began to sweat and so she forced herself to stand so she would stay awake, but she was shaky on her feet. Swept with sudden nausea and light-headedness, she made her way back out to the guest house. Feeling suffocatingly weak and ill, she lay down on the bathroom floor. Then she threw up ... again ... and again.

The last of his guests were departing and still Alfred had not caught sight of Sarah anywhere. The thought that perhaps she was waiting for him in his rooms intoxicated him. While he bid goodnight to the wife of the chairman of a Japanese export outfit, he thought about making love to Sarah, being inside her and bringing her to orgasm over and over again. His sweet Sarah. Perhaps he should marry her after all and think about having another child—perhaps his dream of fatherhood was not yet over. But where could she be?

Desperate to get away from the lingering guests, Alfred

invited them to stay as long as they wished. Then, pleading an early-morning appointment, he bid them good night.

He made his way up the stairs, and not used to being so out of control, Alfred's passion turned to fury when he didn't find Sarah there. How dare she tease him this way. . . .

"Alfred?"

Not Sarah's voice, but comforting, wanting, and familiar.

"Come in, my dear Christine. I had thought you would go out to the pool. It's so hot tonight." His eyes never left her face. He was reading her.

"Hot, yes."

"Lawton didn't make it. Is everything okay?"

Christine's teal blue eyes filled with sudden, shocking tears. "Christine, tell me, what is it, how can I help?"

His tenderness would have shocked most people. But in a crisis, Alfred was a wonderful friend. "I've never known you to be the crying kind." He smiled his ugly smile at her and she felt vaguely comforted.

"It's Lawton and it's me and it's everything. I wish I could do my life all over again."

"I don't. You might write my part out. That would be terrible to me." Her scent was familiar and it tugged at his memory. His anger at Sarah abated as he let Christine in.

Sarah woke up two hours later. She looked in the mirror. Her face was now devoid of all makeup, her cheeks drained of color, the front of her dress stained with vomit.

She wandered back toward the main house, and made her way up to Alfred's bedroom. The door was partly open.

They stood naked, pressed together, kissing. Their tongues were thrusting and exploring each other gluttonously. Then, she watched Christine drop to her knees, taking Alfred into her mouth.

Sarah shivered and clenched her eyes tightly shut. What

was she going to do? She needed Alfred. She was seized by a sickening fear. Helplessness was not a new experience to her. It was a fog without shape or definition, a thick prison to entrap and hold her. What was she going to do?

CHAPTER 25

*I*t was the middle of the season in Palm Beach, but to Christine it felt like her last days—gloomy, depressing, and fraught with a sense of foreboding. In the early evening shadows, lights glowed softly within the house. She had just returned from Alexandra's wing, and tucking her in. She stared at the bank statements on her desk. Keeping up with their friends was tearing away at her nerves and made monthly accounting a torment. She looked haggard and pale, and dark circles formed under her eyes. Lawton had suggested they sell their house and move into something smaller because of their financial troubles. She stared out at her huge oyster-white living room, gave a quick, convulsive shudder, and rose.

She still could not believe that he had quit his job at the bank. She still could not believe that he was preaching for a living. She still could not believe that he insisted they must prove to his congregation that they were just an ordinary, simple couple with simple needs. The man posed riddles of personality more mystifying than she had ever encountered. His insane actions had forced her to go to her own savings. Losing all her hard-earned money, along with her social position, shook her to her toes. Their arguments were coming with phenomenal speed, and as she paced, she felt filled with a slowly mounting, terrifying sensation. The truly frightening part was that they were fairly evenly matched in strength of character and in their ability to impose their wills on each other. They were engaged in a duel, a battle for power and dominance over each other, and their lifestyle. She knew their marriage was near collapse.

Lawton's magnetism rolled over the congregation and they were his within minutes. Once the heat started in him, there was no stopping him. The power took over, the words spilled out. He was smiling in his heartwarming way, and urging the people to praise the Lord. He felt an exorbitant stiffening against his undershorts. He had been speaking for a few months now. He had tasted the power of controlling a crowd, of manipulating them. They were bewildered, hopeful faces—lost little children who needed to be led. He wanted this power again and again. His reputation as a charismatic preacher was spreading. He was persuasive. He could make people cry and *he* could cry. He liked hypnotizing people and making them believe. It was a mirage, an illusion. It was power. And he was making a fortune at it as well, siphoning off millions from the church's discretionary funds. He loved the challenge of talking these boring white-haired dowagers out of their money. Down the road, with his power and money, he would be able to come out of the closet, and be with his lover Harry. That was his true goal.

"Christine, darling, I'm home."

She walked out into the front hallway, prepared for his anger for not showing up at church this evening.

"Hello, sweetheart. Mrs. Avery felt a little faint at the service, so I brought her home to have a bite to eat with us . . . maybe some broth would be nice," Lawton said with commanding gentleness, as he led the old woman to a chair.

Christine watched in amazement as he sat her down. There was something in his voice that was so caring, so benign. Did anyone but she know that it was all manufactured?

"How long has Alexandra been asleep?" he asked.

"For over an hour," Christine replied. She turned to the guest. "Would you care for some soup, Mrs. Avery?"

Throughout the meal Lawton stared at Mrs. Avery with the most grave and patient concern.

"Your husband is a wonderful man, Christine. You're a very fortunate woman."

"Yes, I am," Christine murmured after a brief silence.

"Your chauffeur will be here any minute," Lawton said, giving her his smoothest grin.

"Well, here is a little something for your church, Lawton. I can't thank you enough for taking such good care of me this evening and always." She pressed a check into his hand, for one hundred thousand dollars.

"I promise you I will see that it goes to the worthiest of causes," he said tenderly.

He smiled to himself as he bade her good-bye. He had been working on her for months, and it had finally paid off.

No sooner was the front door shut behind Mrs. Avery than Lawton's entire demeanor changed, his face seeming to be covered in the blackest shadow.

"Don't you ever embarrass me like that again by not showing up for my sermon!" In his eyes was something wild, a strange expression that made Christine afraid.

"I'm going to be someone very important, Christine, and you are not going to get in my way."

"Well, I'm not selling the house or the hotel, Lawton. . . . I don't care what you say!"

"You are not going to ruin my plans!" he shouted, seizing a vase and flinging it to the floor. It burst into a rain of glass.

"What are you staring at?" he snapped.

"What's the matter with you, Lawton? None of this makes sense."

"You must follow my plan." His voice was so hostile, it was like an incision.

"But I don't understand your plan."

"I don't give a damn if you understand or not. We are selling this house!" he screamed. "Without me, you're a nobody, from nowhere. You'll do as I say or have nothing again."

"You're sick. You should see a psychiatrist."

"You ungrateful bitch!"

Shaking with terror, he swung blindly and struck her in the face.

She screamed, from physical terror, from the explosion of the impact, and fell to the floor. She hit the side of the coffee table, her head striking the corner. A single drop of blood slithered slowly from the surface wound.

Neither dared move for a second. They looked at each other as if they could not believe what had happened. Her eyes implored him with the despairing plea of an innocent prisoner. His face was frozen in unreachable determination.

Suddenly, she sprang to her feet and ran toward the stairs, in a panic to escape. She found herself in her dressing room, fumbling, frantically, to lock the door. She stood in the middle of the room, unable to grasp what action she should take. Fear pierced her to her bones. Then her knees gently gave way, and she sank to the floor, shaking.

She heard the front door slam. She did not know how long she sat there on the floor of her dressing room. Her mind was working in broken spurts. She thought of the gun next to the bed that he had given her for protection.

Finally, she made her way to the phone.

Kate pounded on the door.

"It's me, Christine . . . open up."

The door opened slowly.

"Jesus Christ, what's going on?" Kate seized her friend's shoulder in a steadying grasp.

"He hit me."

"I'll be right back . . . sit down."

Kate returned immediately with ice wrapped in a dish towel. She held it up to Christine's head. None of this totally surprised Kate. She had known for years there was something distinctly out of sync with Lawton. She didn't know if he was dangerously disturbed or just a colossal prick. He projected such honesty, when, in fact, he was a master of psychological manipulation. Christine never saw through him, or wanted to. She was too caught up in the social bullshit, the imbecilic illusion of trying to fit into Palm Beach.

Christine's eyes were still and changeless. There was such naked sadness in her face.

"He listed the house with Sotheby's," she began, a quiver in her voice. "He starts every sentence with 'in the spirit of the Lord.' We didn't even get invited to the ball at the Breakers," her exhausted voice trailed off into a sigh. "Or to the Glubman party."

Kate handed her a Kleenex. "They're all social-climbing dimwits from God knows where anyway. What do you care?"

"And now he hit me."

For Christine, there was no shred of sense in any of it, and no point in seeking explanations. Then, without warning, she became hysterical, all the pent-up emotions and stress bursting out in heartbreaking sobs. She trembled with hatred. She had hated her father. She had hated Ned. Now she hated Lawton. She was embittered at the cruel hand fate had dealt her. She was maddened by hatred.

Tears streamed down her face.

What was she going to do? What she indelibly remembered about Lawton was his truly awesome tenderness in the beginning. His vehemence this evening had shocked and startled her. How could this compassionate person have become such a living terror? She had seen him as a savior—now he was going to be her destroyer.

She knew she had to get out of this marriage. She could

either surrender or fight. He would kill her or she would kill him.

Then it struck her.

"Kate, I'm going to Alfred . . . he'll take care of me."

CHAPTER 26

Sarah had been walking aimlessly for hours. She had been drinking all day, downing at least four glasses of wine at a sidewalk cafe on Worth Avenue.

What should she do? She had been thinking about this for days. Alfred had said he would *never* marry again. And even if Garrison were to leave Kate, it wasn't what Sarah wanted. She wanted to stop betraying Kate. She felt trapped. She wished her father were here. She wished a few rays from her sunny childhood would shine through.

She returned home and called Alfred.

"I have to talk to you," she said. "Face to face." She drew a breath. "It's urgent."

"All right, just let me finish my meeting and I'll be right over."

Not an hour later he was in her living room.

"What is it? What's wrong, Sarah?"

He took her hands in his. And his eyes reflected his concern.

She looked down at the floor.

"I'm pregnant, Alfred."

"What?" Comprehension spread slowly across his face. "Is it mine?"

"I haven't been with anyone else in months . . ." she began, plunging into the feeble fabrication.

The room throbbed with silence.

"I'm sorry . . . I was on the pill, but . . . it's an accident. . . ."

"Well, I think we should open a bottle of champagne and celebrate. Everything will be fine, Sarah. I will take care of you, I promise."

She felt her spirit flood with relief and joy.

For the next hour he made a glorious fuss over her. Things were going to work out. Her plan had succeeded. They toasted to the baby, but then Alfred's mood underwent a subtly disturbing change. The excitement fled, and a strange sadness stole into his face. She could not know that Alfred was seeing the face of his son, the boy he would never be able to see or touch again.

"Alfred? You okay?"

"I'm fine, Sarah. Just thinking." He got up and walked to the door. "I must get back to the office. I'll call and check in on you later."

"Alfred?" She nuzzled his cheek.

"Hmm?"

"I love you," she whispered, almost meaning it.

Buoyed by Alfred's assurances and the champagne, Sarah felt happier than in a long while.

She wouldn't have to worry about money anymore. She wouldn't have to try and get into her mother's good graces. Alfred hadn't mentioned marriage, but he had said he would take care of her. The situation wasn't perfect, but it could be possible to have a good relationship. He would take care of her financially; he would bring her security and she would bring him youth.

She smiled contentedly. Finally her past, which had left a trail of horrible black smoke, could be left behind. She started to doze off.

The phone rang, startling her.

"Hello?"

"Sarah?"

"Yes?"

"It's Lisa."

Sarah winced. It was like a sudden chill wind from a great distance. Lisa was part of a past Sarah wanted buried forever. Everything in it was painful. The two had drifted apart ever since that disastrous night at Vassar.

"Sorry I missed you last month at Kate's party," Lisa began. "She mentioned you as a friend once or twice, and finally I realized you were the same Sarah Potter."

"The one and only," Sarah said with false cheer. "How have you been, Lisa?"

"Oh, fine, fine. But I'm afraid I've got some bad news. That's why I'm calling you now after all this time."

"What bad news?"

"Kate knows about the boy we hit at college that night."

Sarah gasped and clenched the phone. The blood drained from her face, and she took several deep gulps of air to regain her composure. "How did she find out, Lisa? What about our promise?"

"I'm sorry, Sarah. It slipped out one night. You remember what happened when I had even one glass of wine. Nothing's changed. I'm really sorry. I didn't know whether to tell you or not, but—"

"Did you tell her my name?"

"Only your first name . . . but I think she's been doing some digging on her own. I felt you should know, although I don't think she'll tell anyone because I have something on her that you can use if necessary."

Sarah felt nausea pounding in her throat. She couldn't speak, and her fingers gripping the phone were rigid and white-knuckled.

"Sarah? Sarah? Are you there?"

"I've got to go, Lisa." She hung up the phone abruptly, desperation coursing through her. She hurried into the bedroom to do a line of cocaine. She needed to clear her mind, needed to think. She couldn't believe this was happening after all these years. If that scandal got out, she would lose her tenuous hold on the small circle that actually welcomed her in.

She had to get Alfred to act quickly, draw up legal papers to protect her position and the baby.

What little composure she had was fast dissolving. The celebration of earlier was now headed for unknown depths of disaster.

Sarah crumpled to the floor, as if a puppet held on strings had suddenly been released.

CHAPTER 27

ate felt suspended. She couldn't get interested in her
work. Garrison was out of town and she felt lonely in his
absence. Her book *Miracles* had remained on the best-seller
list for eight weeks. She should be thinking of her next book,
but she was devoid of inspiration, and she could no longer
call on Lisa for help.

From the top drawer in her desk, she took out a few pages
of a magazine piece she had published, reread it. It was good;
she was proud of it. She had written it by herself, a long time
ago.

Kate took out a tiny key from underneath a stack of yellow legal pages in her desk and went to her bedroom. Her

filing cabinet was behind her gowns, in the very back of her walk-in closet. She opened the bottom drawer. It was stuffed with manila envelopes labeled in her handwriting, and her diaries, all her day-to-day activities since she had arrived in Florida. She lifted out the coffee-stained, dog-eared manuscript from the "Palm Beach" envelope and began to leaf through it. She knew if she did this book, she would have to tell some very private stories. She would lose some friends . . . but she had to come up with a winner, and soon.

She scanned the chapter on Christine and her arrival on the scene.

If she took out that story on Christine's background, she would need something else. Something big to take its place. And she cherished Christine; she was not one of the friends Kate was willing to lose.

She walked back to her office, sat down at the typewriter, rolled in a sheet of fresh paper, and stared at it for a few seconds. She stared with blank terror, as though the enemy was the piece of paper.

Then she picked up the telephone and dialed Alfred Blum's number.

———

Alfred sat in his library.

Kate Robinson was on her way. He had to sit idly and wait—wait for the unknown to descend upon him. She had said she had information on his son. His emotions were clogged into a still, solid ball. The ringing of the telephone in another room sounded like a scream for help. He jumped.

"Miss Robinson here to see you," his maid announced.

Moments later, Kate took the red leather chair directly to his right.

Kate expected him to offer a drink. He didn't.

Alfred expected friendly chitchat before she got down to business. There was none.

"I've been doing research for my new book and I've come across something about a hit-and-run accident that happened in Poughkeepsie several years ago, involving Lisa Greene, Sarah someone, and a boy whose name was kept out of the papers." She paused, drawing a breath. "The young man had enough heroin in his system to have killed him before the car hit."

Alfred's eyes were steady and changeless, not offering a hint of what he was thinking or feeling, but his heart gave a savage lunge he knew could be perilous at his age. He was trying to put two and two together . . . to capture answers from across a span of years.

Kate's signature with her interviewees had always been brevity, and an innate ability to get to the point with a minimum of polite dancing. She hesitated now, though. His one hand lay on the desktop, and she noticed how still and white it was with a pattern of blue veins that did not seem alive.

"I was wondering about the death of your only son, Mr. Blum . . ." her voice faltered. "I could find very little on the actual accident. It seems the autopsy report disappeared, but one police report did make mention of the heroin and the boy's name."

For a minute, Alfred stared out the window. His expression was one of a man resignedly bearing unbearable pain.

"And I thought I had bought them all off," he muttered. "Yes, Miss Robinson, my son was a heroin addict, but that was no reason for his life to be taken so cruelly, so prematurely. And if you think you can use that information for some tawdry tale, think again. Is that why you came here,

Miss Robinson? To take notes on how an old man deals with the fact that his only son was a heroin addict?"

"I came here because I know who one of the people in the car was, and the first name of the driver. I thought you might be interested."

"After all this time, no, I'm not interested. Justice will best be served by leaving me with my memories of my son before he sought peace in a needle."

"I'm going to use this, Mr. Blum."

"I don't think so. Not if you want your marriage to continue."

"What!" Suddenly Kate's world turned upside down. She had come here hoping to add enough facts to the bits and pieces of the story Lisa had told her one drunken night to paint a vivid portrait of a Palm Beach mogul with a terrible family sin—great fodder for a book. And her own investigative efforts had discovered the buried, but not destroyed, police report. For Alfred Blum to now be threatening her made no sense, and yet it scared her as nothing else could.

"You see, your husband has been having an affair with your good friend Sarah . . . the whole town knows that. But what the whole town doesn't know yet is that Sarah is pregnant."

Ice water flooded through her veins.

"I would imagine if Garrison thought he was the father, that might cause a slight problem in your marriage." He now had a mean glint in his eye. "Would he want to stand by her and divorce you?"

Her heart shriveled at those words.

A possessiveness charged through her.

The ball of emotion in her stomach was jealousy.

"Everyone knows how Garrison would feel about an heir
... you might lose your husband."

Jealousy consumed her utterly. She held onto the strange
feeling, trying to understand. It was not pleasant. She suddenly realized that losing her husband was a strong possibility. Her heart gave a lurch.

"Am I talking too fast for you, Miss Robinson?" His eyes
flashed warfare.

"You see ... Kate ... you must never, ever underestimate
your opponents." His voice was raspy and ugly, and a
strange kind of triumphant smile crumpled his face.

Kate felt the thin outer layer of her facade begin to crack
as she raced out of the room.

CHAPTER 28

$\mathcal{N}$ed had returned from a fishing trip to Canada last evening. He had gone away to think, especially about Jessie. When he entered his home, the walls seemed to swallow him, suffocating him as if in a trap. He felt anger. The anger a man feels when a woman begins to bind him. The anger a man feels when he wants to run off. The divorce papers he had his lawyer draw up lay on the desk before him. He sat staring at them, hunched by hatred. He knew he had fallen fathomlessly in love with Jessie.

It was just after midnight, and Jessie had just finished a painting for Allison and propped it on a little table easel next to her bed, ready to surprise her when she woke up.

She stared at her sleeping daughter, filled, as always, with joy at the sight of her. Unlike the pool of misery she had been swimming in over the last few weeks, she was now flushed with high spirits. Allison did that for her. She touched her hair lightly. She looked so serene and beautiful, it brought a lump to her throat.

A few days ago, with Ned away, a quiet and happy kind of closure occurred within Jessie because she had made a decision. She was not going to get sucked toward the epicenter of another destructive relationship. She had decided to end it. She finally had the courage to reclaim the scattered pieces of her life, and compose a new one.

She returned to her studio, energy flowing from her. She was concentrating on a new painting when suddenly she had that shadowed sense that there was someone in the room with her. She was aware of him sitting on the window ledge, watching.

"Ned!"

"The window was open. . . ."

"But why didn't you ring the doorbell?"

"I wanted to surprise . . . I just wanted to watch you . . . look at you. . . ."

"Ned, you're not making any sense."

"Jessie, will you marry me?"

He held her eyes.

"It's too late," she whispered after a long silence. "Nobody will ever be able to take our good memories from us, Ned, but I've decided we're not good for each other."

He felt close to an insanity of desire for her.

He walked toward her. He filled his hands with her breasts. He buried his face between them.

"I can't lose you. . . . I'll make you love me. I'll get a

divorce. I will, I promise." His voice was charged with emotion.

"It won't work, Ned . . . not for me." Jessie thought with a terrible sadness how happy those words would have made her such a short time ago. But now nothing would ever be the same. Their passion had helped free her from the prison of her childhood and released her from the memories, like terrorists, which held her hostage. But it seemed that the moment Ned returned her to herself, he needed to strip her apart. How could she ever trust his loving again? Even now, her knees shook at the thought of how close he was and how much he had hurt her the last time they made love. She feared she might die if he made love to her again, that she might slip away just like the happy childhood that had died with her father.

He held her arm tightly in his grasp, then began to grope. He was going to have her, there and then. A table fell over. . . .

"No . . . no. . . . Please don't. Stop it, Ned! Stop it!"

The look on his face hit her with the abruptness of a collision. It was a mask, withered and pitiable.

"I want to make love to you now."

"No, that won't save us, Ned," she pleaded.

His grip became tighter.

She struggled free.

Then there was an animal scream of terror.

CHAPTER 29

$\mathcal{B}$oth sides of the road in front of the Episcopal church, and the side streets, were filled with cars, and the church itself was crowded beyond capacity. There was very little made in the obituary columns about the accidental drowning. However, the idea of him being home all day alone, found accidentally by the maid, lingering a few days without regaining consciousness, created a momentary excitement in town.

Great baskets of yellow and white hyacinths were on either side of the altar. An enormous spray of white orchids was placed on the table with the antique Tiffany vase that held his ashes.

Once seated, Kate bowed her head in prayer, and got lost in her own thoughts. Happiness had almost been ripped from her grasp. There were still adjustments to make, but the will was there. Both she and Garrison wanted badly to make the marriage work. She knew she could never be totally straightforward in the recital of her past. Garrison had told her he was very aware she indulged in certain evasions, but he didn't care, he simply adored her. And she finally agreed to adopt a child.

Christine sat in a middle row, next to a stranger, gazing out the rose-stained glass window, fanning herself. She looked beautiful.

She thought back to when she had first come to Palm Beach. She thought of the night she found out Mark was really Ned Cooper. She thought about all the times she had agonized over running into him after that. How she had always dropped her eyes, hoping he would do the same. However, he hardly glanced at her, and if their eyes accidentally connected, there had never been a trace of remorse or guilt in his demeanor. His mask of impassivity was his classic defense.

"Aren't the flowers lovely?"

She heard the words but moved on with her own thoughts about her recent divorce from Lawton. How tired she had gotten of his preaching. And how tired she had gotten with keeping up the front of having a good marriage.

She remembered now how Lawton's face would turn murky with rage. She remembered how he howled, his voice rising in wild, uncontained anger. His capacity for destruction had been awful. He was talented enough at delusion that he could create a facade of decency that bore no relation to reality.

She glanced around at the large congregation. Trying to fit in here had been a foolish mistake. She could not believe that this was the society she had so reverently looked up to, and so eagerly learned to join. She had climbed a mountain toward a foggy shape that had loomed like a castle . . . and had found it to be a gutted house. Everybody had their skeletons. Another lie, another fantasy, another facade, served up to provide a barrier.

Christine straightened her back until it was not touching the seat. She felt a fierce certainty that she would survive here, as she always had.

Sarah sat very still, her hands clasped delicately over her stomach. Any day now her pregnancy would start to show. She had begun the painful steps of alcohol and drug withdrawal, and if sometimes she slipped, at least there was a reason to try harder the next time. Her baby needed her and Alfred wanted her. And the past would become eclipsed by these two people who would build her future.

Sarah hated funerals and so she only half listened to the eulogy as she looked around. Christine appeared even more beautiful since leaving Lawton. Their divorce had been rocket-fast and Sarah knew Alfred had pulled strings on Christine's behalf. But Sarah was no longer put off by Christine so much as she admired her.

Sarah had come far in forgiveness. Though she believed her family had failed her, she wasn't angry anymore. She had made friends who meant much to her—enough to be strong about Garrison, enough to protect Kate. And though Kate was angry, they shared enough between them to work their friendship out. Kate, too, was responsible, and admitted it.

And the ugly older man beside her genuinely loved her. While Alfred still clung to his fear of marriage, the baby would have his name and his support and that's what mattered. Maria believed he would come around. And she, Sarah, would stop being patched together and finally be whole. She was sure of it.

———

Jessie sat unobtrusively in the last pew of the church. Her hair was pulled back, her eyes hidden by dark sunglasses. She bowed her head in prayer. Overwhelming thoughts of the past pushed the prayers from her mind. Too many thoughts to sort out.

She felt a tinge of negativity—a small hard point of fear. It was the distant headlight advancing upon her down the invisible track.

She momentarily thought of Jake. All that was left in her memory of that marriage was a blurred recollection of a few moments of bliss. Yet, of course, the most important event in her life came from that union—Allison. Allison held out the lifeline to her soul.

A calm and peaceful serenity descended sweetly over her for a second. Then she thought how sad it was that Allison had been pushed out of her childhood, and how the divorce had polluted it. Jessie wished she could reach inside Allison's soul and fix everything, but of course, she knew she couldn't.

The sound of her heartbeat filled her ears. She thought of her childhood. The smothering guilt she carried for allowing her stepfather to touch her. For not being able to stop him.

The headlight moving upon her grew larger. She wiped a

tear away with her finger. She touched the gold Buddha on a chain around her neck. It had been a gift from Ned. She thought back to when they first met, the awkwardness, the sexual pleasure.

There was a little smile of remembrance on her lips. She thought of their time together. The five years. Their relationship had ebbed and flowed in majestic waves over the years. Their timing was wrong, yet he had shifted her life; she was forever changed because of him.

The service ended with a simple prayer. The widow stood up and started to walk down the aisle.

Mrs. Ned Cooper stared straight ahead. She saw Jessie, but she gave no sign of it. Nothing penetrated the stoic calm of the widow. She did not want to be embarrassed by any scandal . . . and she certainly wanted the Cooper fortune intact. The home she had shared with Ned had been nothing more than a magnificent movie set for a performance. The divorce papers she had found on the desk were now nothing but ashes . . . the same as her husband.

Detective Gus Smith stood in the back of the church watching the large congregation of mourners. How does a man in perfectly good health trip and fall into his own pool? The circumstances were bizarre. The idea of foul play began to nag at him, even though there wasn't any hard evidence. No one in his house saw anything. The wife was in Europe, so she was clear even though he found divorce papers not yet filed or signed. Jessie admitted Ned had come over that night, but left her house at around midnight; she never left the house that evening.

He had had lots of business enemies. The report from the hospital said there was a blow to the right back side of the head. It could have been from the edge of the pool, but something about that didn't ring true with Gus. And why was the body cremated so quickly? That bewildered him.

He looked at all the faces and wondered about all the skeletons in the church. Nobody goes through life unscathed. Everybody has their struggles, their own dark places. Even the rich.

As the people left the church, they scrutinized him. He smiled to himself. He knew he stood out here; no one else was the color of fudge.

Gus drove from the church directly to Maria's house. If she couldn't help him, he had nothing to go on, and he might have to give up on this one.

"Hello, Gus," Maria greeted him.

"May I come in?"

"Of course."

He held a sterling silver candlestick holder in his right hand.

"Coffee?"

"Yes, thanks."

"I took this out of Jessie's studio," he began, setting it on the kitchen table. "It's clean as a whistle."

Maria's heart gave a lurch. She looked to see that he was gazing straight into her eyes.

"I know she's a friend of yours. . . . It's just a hunch I have that something is not right in the Cooper case."

Maria raised her eyebrows in an arch of surprise meant to disguise the fear she felt. For a moment she did not trust herself to speak. He would not be here unless he suspected something other than accidental drowning.

"Leave it here with me, Gus," she said. "Come by in the morning."

"When did you see her last?"

"I haven't seen her in weeks," she said, walking him outside. She was standing in the sunlight, but suddenly she was chilled.

———

For the remainder of the day and into the evening, Maria walked around the silver candlestick holder. She did not touch it. Oh, how she loved Jessie. Yet, she was so complicated. It was very difficult for anyone to gain a thorough picture of Jessie, especially of her childhood and youth.

The look in Maria's face was a wistful longing, as if seeing Jessie from a great distance. She was straining and failing to get closer.

She held her breath for a moment, then picked up the silver candlestick holder. Her hand froze. The vision was suddenly exceptionally clear.

Maria could see Jessie standing in Allison's room, watching her sleep. Jessie stood there smiling at her daughter with such an unbearable love. Maria was inside Jessie seeing life as she sees it, hearing it as she hears it, feeling it as she feels it. Jessie stood there without any of her barriers; her barriers of guilt, anger, judgments were gone. She was the pure essence of a mother's love.

Maria stepped backward for a second. She could feel Jessie so totally, and she was not strong enough at that instant to take such undiluted love.

Then she saw Jessie go back to her studio. Ned was there waiting for her. They started to have an argument over their relationship.

Ned came forward with his arms outstretched and pinned her against the wall.

He was pushing himself sexually on her, thinking it was an immediate answer to their problems. Jessie was imploring him to stop. He was panting heavily. He was a mixture of emotions: lust, love, resentment. For Jessie, it was one of those rare moments in life when a feeling she thought she had buried came heaving to the surface.

Maria shook her head. For some reason things went foggy on her. Why?

A hand reached for the candlestick . . . and swung. There was blood on his shirt, blood on the floor, then he fell backward. Ned blacked out, but only briefly, then he got up. He went home. She could see him pacing by his pool, once again getting very excited by the thought of losing Jessie. Again, he blacked out, this time falling into the pool. He was floating face down in the water. He was the King of Spades.

Maria needed to lie down. The scene she had just been a participant in had exhausted her. She knew there was nothing she could do to alter the fate Jessie embraced.

What should be her own path? Should she tell Gus what she knew?

She stared at the ceiling, stained with the shadows of the night. She wondered how one mortal human being could be the vessel to contain such monumental guilt. Maria knew the soul would be purified by the pain. Did Jessie? She let out a cry, wrenched from the dungeon of her soul.

She could not hurt Jessie. She thought of the love she had witnessed between mother and daughter. She could see the two of them smiling at each other as if they shared some glorious secret.

With all the power in her soul, in this life and beyond,

Maria willed herself to accept the truth. Above her loomed a glorious creature that glowed with spiritual beauty. Behind, there were faces, hands beckoning her quietly, a few sparkling lights like smiles of welcome.

Maria understood her path was finished here. As she fell into her endless sleep, the last piece of the puzzle was given to her, and accepted by her, accepted because she knew she would never have to share it.

That last piece was Allison's hand on the candlestick . . . not Jessie's.

Acknowledgments

Thank you to Jean for all of your willingness to help throughout your own difficult year.

Thank you to M.W., my dear friend, for all of your wisdom along the way.

Thank you to Susanne Jaffe, my editor, for supporting, enduring, and helping me from beginning to end.